The Welsh Fairy Book

W. Jenkyn Thomas

DOVER PUBLICATIONS, INC.
Mineola, New York

Copyright

Bibliographical Note

This Dover edition, first published in 2001, is an unabridged reprint of the text of *The Welsh Fairy Book,* which was originally published by Frederick A. Stokes, Co., New York, 1907.

Library of Congress Cataloging-in-Publication Data

Thomas, W. Jenkyn (William Jenkyn)
The Welsh fairy book / W. Jenkyn Thomas.
p. cm.
Reprint. Originally published New York : Frederick A. Stokes Co., 1907
Summary: A collection of eighty-three fairy tales and folk tales from Wales, including The Lady of the Lake, The Fairy Harp, Pennard Castle, and The Stray Cow.
ISBN 0-486-41711-5 (pbk.)
1. Fairy Tales—Wales. [1. Fairy tales. 2. Folklore—Wales.] I. Title.

PZ8.T3655 We 2001
398.2'09429—dc21

00-052366

Manufactured in the United States of America
Dover Publications, Inc., 31 East 2nd Street, Mineola, N.Y. 11501

To
Mimi, Billie and Jack

Contents

Preface

THIS book has been prepared for youthful readers in general, and for Welsh boys and girls in particular.

I found, when schoolmastering in South Wales, that all the fairy books in the school library were in such constant demand that they rapidly wore out. This led me to inquire whether the readers were familiar with the fairy mythology of their own country. While, however, they were learned in the folk-lore of other nations, they were, with few exceptions, ignorant of the Fair Family and other legends of Wales. Further inquiries convinced me that boys and girls throughout Wales were generally in the same case.

When remonstrated with, my pupils excused themselves on the ground that no Welsh fairy stories had been related to them, and that there was no handy collection which they could read. On reflection, I had to recognise that there was much more justice in this plea than in the vast majority of excuses with which I had to deal. The practice of narrating fairy stories has certainly almost died out in Wales, and strange as it may appear in these days when young readers are so lavishly catered for, it is a fact that no Welsh fairy book has been compiled for boys and girls. After waiting in vain for a more competent editor to undertake the work, I have prepared this book, primarily with the object of depriving Welsh school children of the defence put forward by my quondam disciples, but at the same time hoping that the Welsh variants of the universal folk-tales will interest a wider circle of readers.

The sources of the stories are many and diverse in character:

for example, "Elidyr's Sojourn in Fairy-Land" is taken from Giraldus Cambrensis: "Einion and the Lady of the Greenwood" hails from the Iolo MSS.: while "The Drowning of the Bottom Hundred" comes, stripped of its irony, from Thomas Love Peacock's "Misfortune's of Elphin." Here it may be remarked that the style of the originals has been left largely untouched.

I have been kindly permitted by Sir John Rhys and the Delegates of the Oxford University Press to make use of "Celtic Folk-Lore: Welsh and Manx" (it would be difficult to exaggerate the value to the scientific folk-lorist of this great thesaurus): of Elias Owen's "Welsh Folk-Lore," by Messrs. Woodall, Minshall, Thomas & Co.' Oswestry: of Wirt Sikes's "British Goblins," by Messrs. Sampson Low, Marston & Co.: of "Bedd Gelert: Its Facts, Fairies and Folk-Lore," by the Rev. D. E. Jenkins: of "The Curse of Pantannas" and "The Llanfabon Changeling," by Mr. Isaac Craigfryn Hughes. My warmest thanks are due to the above for their courtesy.

It may be as well to add that, while in some stories it has been necessary to piece scraps together, nothing has been inserted that is not genuinely traditionary.

Notes on Welsh Pronunciation

Welsh pronunciation is not nearly so difficult as it is popularly supposed to be. With the exception of *y*, every letter has an invariable value, and is always pronounced.

VOWELS.

a short:	pronounced	as in p*a*n.
a long	”	” f*a*ther.
e short	”	” p*e*n.
e long	”	like the first element of the diphthong in l*a*ne.
i short	”	as in p*i*n.
i long	”	” mach*i*ne.
o short	”	” c*o*t.
o long	”	like the first element of the diphthong in n*o*te.
u	”	(approximately) like the French *u* in s*u*r.
w short	”	like the *oo* in w*oo*d.
w long	”	” ” w*oo*ed.
y	”	sometimes like *u* in b*u*t, and sometimes (approximately) like the French *u* in s*u*r.

DIPHTHONGS.

They may be pronounced by giving to each of the component vowels the value indicated above.

CONSONANTS.

c is always pronounced as *k, ch* as in the Scotch lo*ch, dd* as *th* in brea*the*, *f* as *v*, *ff* as *f, s* is always hard, as in lo*ss; ll* represents a spirant *l*, a very difficult sound to represent in English—Englishmen generally render it as *thl*.

ACCENT.

The accent is nearly always on the last syllable but one (or penult) as Elídyr, Seithényn.

EXAMPLES.

Gwyddno = Gwithno, th as in breathe; Gwenhúdiw = Gwenhíd-ue; Syfáddon = Syváthon, th as in breathe; Dwt = Dŏŏt, oo as in wood; Pwca = Pŏŏka, oo as in wood; Ardúdwy = Ardídŏŏi; Llwyd = Llōōid, ll the spirant l, oo as in wooed.

The Lady of the Lake

HIGH up in a hollow of the Black Mountains of South Wales is a lonely sheet of water called Llyn y Fan Fach.

In a farm not far from this lake there lived in the olden time a widow, with an only son whose name was Gwyn. When this son grew up, he was often sent by his mother to look after the cattle grazing. The place where the sweetest food was to be found was near the lake, and it was thither that the mild-eyed beasts wandered whenever they had their will. One day when Gwyn was walking along the banks of the mere, watching the kine cropping the short grass, he was astonished to see a lady standing in the clear smooth water, some distance from the land.

She was the most beautiful creature that he had ever set eyes upon, and she was combing her long hair with a golden comb, the unruffled surface of the lake serving her as a mirror.

He stood on the brink, gazing fixedly at the maiden, and straightway knew that he loved her. As he gazed, he unconsciously held out to her the barley-bread and cheese which his mother had given him before he left home. The lady gradually glided towards him, but shook her head as he continued to hold out his hand, and saying:

Cras dy fara,	O thou of the crimped bread,
Nid hawdd fy nala,	It is not easy to catch me,

she dived under the water, and disappeared from his sight.

He went home, full of sorrow, and told his mother of the beautiful vision which he had seen. As they pondered over the strange words used by the mysterious lady before she plunged out of sight, they came to the conclusion that there must have been some spell connected with the hard-baked bread, and the mother advised her son to take with him some "toes," or unbaked dough, when next he went to the lake.

Next morning, long before the sun appeared above the crest of the mountain, Gwyn was by the lake with the dough in his hand, anxiously waiting for the Lady of the Lake to appear above the surface. The sun rose, scattering with his powerful beams the mists which veiled the high ridges around, and mounted high in the heavens. Hour after hour the youth watched the waters, but hour after hour there was nothing to be seen except the ripples raised by the breeze and the sunbeams dancing upon them. By the late afternoon despair had crept over the watcher, and he was on the point of turning his footsteps homeward when to his intense delight the lady again appeared above the sunlit ripples. She seemed even more beautiful than before, and Gwyn, forgetting in admiration of her fairness all that he had carefully prepared to say, could only hold out his hand, offering to her the dough. She refused the gift with a shake of the head as before, adding the words:

Llaith dy fara,	O thou of the moist bread,
Ti ni fynna.	I will not have thee.

Then she vanished under the water, but before she sank out of sight, she smiled upon the youth so sweetly and so graciously that his heart became fuller than ever of love. As he walked home slowly and sadly, the remembrance of her smile consoled him and awakened the hope that when next she appeared she would not refuse his gift. He told his mother what had happened, and she advised him, inasmuch as the lady had refused both hard-baked and unbaked bread, to take with him next time bread that was half-baked.

That night he did not sleep a wink, and long before the first twilight he was walking the margin of the lake with half-baked bread in his hand, watching its smooth surface even more impatiently than the day before.

The sun rose and the rain came, but the youth heeded nothing as he eagerly strained his gaze over the water. Morning wore to afternoon, and afternoon to evening, but nothing met the eyes of the anxious watcher but the waves and the myriad dimples made in them by the rain. The shades of night began to fall, and Gwyn was about to depart in sore disappointment, when, casting a last farewell look over the lake, he beheld some cows walking on its surface. The sight of these beasts made him hope that they would be followed by the Lady of the Lake, and, sure enough, before long the maiden emerged from the water. She seemed lovelier than ever, and Gwyn was almost beside himself with joy at her appearance. His rapture increased when he saw that she was gradually approaching the land, and he rushed into the water to meet her, holding out the half-baked bread in his hand. She, smiling, took his gift, and allowed him to lead her to dry land. Her beauty dazzled him, and for some time he could do nothing but gaze upon her. And as he gazed upon her he saw that the sandal on her right foot was tied in a peculiar manner. She smiled so graciously upon him that he at last recovered his speech and said, "Lady, I love you more than all the world besides and want you to be my wife."

She would not consent at first. He pleaded, however, so earnestly that she at last promised to be his bride, but only on the following condition. "I will wed you," she said, "and I will live with you until I receive from you three blows without a cause—tri ergyd diachos. When you strike me the third causeless blow I will leave you for ever."

He was protesting that he would rather cut off his hand than employ it in such a way, when she suddenly darted from him and dived into the lake. His grief and disappointment was so sore that he determined to put an end to his life by casting himself headlong into the deepest water of the lake. He rushed to the top of a great rock overhanging the water, and was on the point of jumping in when he heard a loud voice saying, "Forbear, rash youth, and come hither."

He turned and beheld on the shore of the lake some distance from the rock a hoary-headed old man of majestic mien, accompanied by two maidens. He descended from the rock in fear and trembling, and the old man addressed him in comforting accents.

"Mortal, thou wishest to wed one of these my daughters. I will consent to the union if thou wilt point out to me the one thou lovest."

Gwyn gazed upon the two maidens, but they were so exactly similar in stature, apparel and beauty that he could not see the slightest difference between them. They were such perfect counterparts of each other that it seemed quite impossible to say which of them had promised to be his bride, and the thought that if perchance he fixed upon the wrong one all would be for ever lost nearly drove him to distraction. He was almost giving up the task in despair when one of the two maidens very quietly thrust her foot slightly forward. The motion, simple as it was, did not escape the attention of the youth, and looking down he saw the peculiar shoe-tie which he had observed on the sandal of the maiden who had accepted his half-baked bread. He went forward and boldly took hold of her hand.

"Thou hast chosen rightly," said the old man, "be to her a kind and loving husband, and I will give her as a dowry as many sheep, cattle, goats, swine and horses as she can count of each without drawing in her breath. But remember, if thou strikest her three causeless blows, she shall return to me."

Gwyn was overjoyed, and again protested that he would rather lop off all his limbs than do such a thing. The old man smiled, and turning to his daughter desired her to count the number of sheep she wished to have. She began to count by fives—one, two, three, four, five—one, two, three, four, five—one, two, three, four, five—as many times as she could until her breath was exhausted. In an instant as many sheep as she had counted emerged from the water. Then the father asked her to count the cattle she desired. One, two, three, four, five—one, two, three, four, five—one, two, three, four, five—she went on counting until she had to draw in her breath again. Without delay, black cattle to the number she had been able to reach came lowing out of the mere. In the same way she counted the goats, swine and horses she wanted, and the full tale of each kind ranged themselves alongside the sheep and cattle. Then the old man and his other daughter vanished.

The Lady of the Lake and Gwyn were married amid great rejoicing, and took up their home at a farm named Esgair Llaethdy, where they lived for many years. They were as happy as happy can be, everything prospered with them, and three sons were born to them.

When the eldest boy was seven years old, there was a wedding some distance away, to which Nelferch—for that was the name the Lady of the Lake gave herself—and her husband were specially invited. When the day came, the two started and were walking through a field in which some of their horses were grazing, when Nelferch said that the distance was too great for her to walk and she would rather not go. "We must go," said her husband, "and if you do not like to walk, you can ride one of these horses. Do you catch one of them while I go back to the house for the saddle and bridle."

"I will," she said. "At the same time bring me my gloves. I have forgotten them—they are on the table."

He went back to the house, and when he returned with the saddle and bridle and gloves he found to his surprise that she had not stirred from the spot where he had left her. Pointing to the horses, he playfully flicked her with the gloves and said, "Go, go (dos, dos)."

"This is the first causeless blow," she said with a sigh, and reminded him of the condition upon which she had married him, a condition which he had almost forgotten.

Many years after, they were both at a christening. When all the guests were full of mirth and hilarity, Nelferch suddenly burst into tears and sobbed piteously. Gwyn tapped her on the shoulder and asked her why she wept. "I weep," she said, "because this poor innocent babe is so weak and frail that it will have no joy in this world. Pain and suffering will fill all the days of its brief stay on earth, and in the agony of torture will it depart this life. And, husband, thou hast struck me the second causeless blow."

After this, Gwyn was on his guard day and night not to do anything which could be regarded as a breach of their marriage covenant. He was so happy in the love of Nelferch and his children that he knew his heart would break if through some accident he gave the last and only blow which would take his dear wife from him. Some time after, the babe whose christening they had attended, after a short life of pain and suffering, died in agony, as Nelferch had foretold. Gwyn and the Lady of the Lake went to the funeral, and in the midst of the mourning and grief, Nelferch laughed merrily, causing all to stare at her in astonishment. Her husband was so shocked at her high spirits on so sad an occasion, that he touched her, saying, "Hush, wife, why dost thou laugh?"

"I laugh," she replied, "because the poor babe is at last happy and free from pain and suffering." Then rising she said, "The last blow has been struck. Farewell."

She started off immediately towards Esgair Llaethdy, and when she arrived home, she called her cattle and other stock together, each by name. The cattle she called thus:

Mu wlfrech, moelfrech,	Brindled cow, bold freckled,
Mu olfrech, gwynfrech,	Spotted cow, white speckled,
Pedair cae tonn-frech,	Ye four field sward mottled.
Yr hen wynebwen,	The old white-faced,
A'r las Geigen,	And the grey Geigen
Gyda'r tarw gwyn	With the white bull
O lys y Brenin,	From the court of the King,
A'r llo du bach,	And thou little black calf,
Sydd ar y bach,	Suspended on the hook,
Dere dithe, yn iach adre!	Come thou also, whole again, home.

They all immediately obeyed the summons of their mistress. The little black calf, although it had been killed, came to life again, and descending from the hook, walked off with the rest of the cattle, sheep, goats, swine and horses at the command of the Lady of the Lake.

It was the spring of the year, and there were four oxen ploughing in one of the fields. To these she cried:

Y pedwar edion glas,	Ye four grey oxen,
Sydd ar y ma's,	That are on the field,
Deuwch chwithe	Come you also
Yn iach adre!	Whole and well home!

Away went the whole of the live stock with the Lady across the mountain to the lake from whence they had come, and disappeared beneath its waters. The only trace they left was the furrow made by the plough which the oxen drew after them into the lake; this remains to this day.

Gwyn's heart was broken. He followed his wife to the lake, crushed with woe, and put an end to his misery by plunging into the depths of the cold water. The three sons distracted with grief, almost followed their father's example, and spent most of their days wandering about the lake in the hope of seeing their lost mother once more. Their love was at last rewarded, for one day Nelferch appeared suddenly to them.

She told them that their mission on earth was to relieve the pain and misery of mankind. She took them to a place which is still called the Physician's Dingle (Pant y Meddygon), where she showed them the virtues of the plants and herbs which grew there, and taught them the art of healing.

Profiting by their mother's instruction, they became the most skilful physicians in the land. Rhys Grug, Lord of Llandovery and Dynevor Castles, gave them rank, lands and privileges at Myddfai for their maintenance in the practice of their art and for the healing and benefit of those who should seek their help. The fame of the Physicians of Myddfai was established over the whole of Wales, and continued for centuries among their descendants.

Arthur in the Cave

ONCE upon a time a Welshman was walking on London Bridge, staring at the traffic, and wondering why there were so many kites hovering about. He had come to London after many adventures with thieves and highwaymen, which need not be related here, in charge of a herd of black Welsh cattle. He had sold them with much profit, and with jingling gold in his pocket he was going about to see the sights of the city.

He was carrying a hazel staff in his hand, for you must know that a good staff is as necessary to a drover as teeth are to his dog. He stood still to gaze at some wares in a shop (for at that time London Bridge was shops from beginning to end), when he noticed that a man was looking at his stick with a long fixed look. The man after a while came to him and asked him where he came from. "I come from my own country," said the Welshman, rather surlily, for he could not see what business the man had to ask him such a question.

"Do not take it amiss," said the stranger; "if you will only answer my questions and take my advice, it will be of greater benefit to you than you imagine. Do you remember where you cut that stick?"

The Welshman was still suspicious and said, "What does it matter where I cut it?"

"It matters," said his questioner, "because there is treasure hidden near the spot where you cut that stick. If you remember the place and can conduct me to it, I will put you in possession of great riches."

The Welshman now understood that he had to deal with a sorcerer, and he was greatly perplexed as to what to do. On the one hand, he was tempted by the prospect of wealth; on the other hand, he knew that the sorcerer must have derived his knowledge from devils, and he feared to have anything to do with the powers of darkness. The cunning man strove hard to persuade him, and at length made him promise to show the place where he had cut his hazel staff.

The Welshman and the magician journeyed together to Wales. They went to Craig y Dinas, the Rock of the Fortress, at the head of the Neath Valley, near Pont Nedd Fechan, and the Welshman, pointing to the stock or root of an old hazel, said, "This is where I cut my stick."

"Let us dig," said the sorcerer. They digged until they came to a broad, flat stone. Prising this up, they found some steps leading downwards. They went down the steps and along a narrow passage until they came to a door. "Are you brave," asked the sorcerer, "will you come in with me?"

"I will," said the Welshman, his curiosity getting the better of his fear.

They opened the door, and a great cave opened out before them. There was a faint red light in the cave, and they could see everything. The first thing they came to was a bell. "Do not touch that bell," said the sorcerer, "or it will be all over with us both."

As they went further in, the Welshman saw that the place was not empty. There were soldiers lying down asleep, thousands of them, as far as ever the eye could see. Each one was clad in bright armour, the steel helmet of each was on his head, the shining shield of each was on his arm, the sword of each was near his hand, each had his spear stuck in the ground near him, and each and all were asleep. In the middle of the cave was a great round table at which sat warriors, whose noble features and richly-dight armour proclaimed that they were not in the roll of common men.

Each of those, too, had his head bent down in sleep. On a golden throne on the further side of the round table was a King of gigantic stature and august presence. In his hand, held below the hilt, was a mighty sword with scabbard and haft of gold studded with gleaming gems; on his head was a crown set with precious stones which flashed and glinted like so many points of fire. Sleep had set its seal on his eyelids also.

"Are they asleep?" asked the Welshman, hardly believing his own eyes.

"Yes, each and all of them," answered the sorcerer, "but if you touch yonder bell, they will all awake."

"How long have they been asleep?"

"For over a thousand years!"

"Who are they?"

"Arthur's warriors, waiting for the time to come when they shall destroy all the enemies of the Cymry and repossess the Island of Britain, establishing their own King once more at Caer Lleon."

"Who are those sitting at the round table?"

"Those are Arthur's Knights, Owain, the son of Urien; Cai, the son of Cynyr; Gwalchmai, the son of Gwyar; Peredur, the son of Efrawc; Geraint, the son of Erbin; Trystan, the son of March; Bedwyr, the son of Bedrawd; Cilhwch, the son of Celyddon; Edeyrn, the son of Nudd; Cynon, the son of Clydno"—"And on the golden throne?" broke in the Welshman—"is Arthur himself, with his sword Excalibur in his hand," replied the sorcerer.

Impatient by this time at the Welshman's questions, the sorcerer hastened to a great heap of yellow gold on the floor of the cave. He took up as much as he could carry, and bade his companion do the same. "It is time for us to go," he then said, and he led the way towards the door by which they had entered.

But the Welshman was fascinated by the sight of the countless soldiers in their glittering arms, all asleep. "How I should like to see them all awaking!" he said to himself. "I will touch the bell—I *must* see them all arising from their sleep."

When they came to the bell, he struck it until it rang through the whole place. As soon as it rang, lo! the thousands of warriors leapt to their feet and the ground beneath them shook with the sound of the steel arms. And a great voice came from their midst, "Who rang the bell? Has the day come?"

The sorcerer was so frightened that he shook like an aspen leaf. He shouted in answer, "No, the day has not come. Sleep on."

The mighty host was all in motion, and the Welshman's eyes

were dazzled as he looked at the bright steel arms which illumined the cave as with the light of myriad flames of fire.

"Arthur," said the voice again, "awake; the bell has rung, the day is breaking. Awake, Arthur the Great."

"No," shouted the sorcerer, "it is still night; sleep on, Arthur the Great."

A sound came from the throne. Arthur was standing, and the jewels in his crown shone like bright stars above the countless throng. His voice was strong and sweet like the sound of many waters, and he said, "My warriors, the day has not come when the Black Eagle and the Golden Eagle shall go to war. It is only a seeker after gold who has rung the bell. Sleep on, my warriors, the morn of Wales has not yet dawned."

A peaceful sound like the distant sigh of the sea came over the cave, and in a trice the soldiers were all asleep again. The sorcerer hurried the Welshman out of the cave, moved the stone back to its place, and vanished.

Many a time did the Welshman try to find the way into the cave again, but though he dug over every inch of the hill, he never found the entrance.

The Curse of Pantannas

LONG, long ago, at the farm of Pantannas, in Glamorgan, there lived a churlish old husbandman. He hated the Fair Folk who danced on his fields to the light of the moon, and longed to discover some way of ridding his land of them.

Not being able to think of any plan, he went to an old witch and told her of his wish. She made him promise to give her one night's milking on his farm, and then advised him thus:

"Wherever you see a fairy ring in your fields plough it and sow it with corn," she said. "When the fairies find the greensward gone, they will never revisit the spot."

The farmer took her advice. He yoked his oxen and drove his iron ploughshare through every circle in which the fairies had danced at night, and sowed it with corn. The nightly sounds of dance and song ceased, and no fairy was afterwards seen in the fields of Pantannas.

The farmer rejoiced greatly, imagining vain things, until one evening in the spring of the year, when the wheat was green in the fields. The farmer was returning home in the red light of the setting sun, when a tiny little man in a red coat came to him, unsheathed a little sword, and directing the point towards him, said:

Dial a ddaw,	Vengeance cometh,
Y mae gerllaw.	Fast it approacheth.

After saying this, the mannikin disappeared. The farmer tried to laugh; but there was something in the angry, grim looks of the little man which made him feel very uncomfortable.

Spring, however, turned into summer, and summer into autumn, without anything happening, and the farmer thought that he had been very foolish to fear the threat of the little man in the red coat.

In the autumn, when the corn was golden in the fields and ripe for the sickle, the farmer and his family were one night going to bed. Suddenly they heard a mighty noise, which shook the house as though it would fall. As they trembled with fear, they heard a loud voice saying:

Daw dial. Vengeance cometh.

Next morning, no ear or straw was to be seen in the cornfields, only black ashes. The fairies had burnt all the harvest.

The farmer was walking through his fields, gazing ruefully at the destruction wrought by the fairies, when he was met by the same little man as before. Pointing his sword threateningly, the elf said:

Nid yw ond dechreu. It but beginneth.

The farmer's face turned as white as milk, and he began to plead for pardon. He was quite willing, he said, to allow the fields where the fairies had been wont to dance and sing to grow again into a greensward.

They could dance in their rings as often as they wished without interference, provided only they would punish him no more.

"No," was the stern reply. "The word of the King has gone forth that he will avenge himself on thee, and no power can recall it."

The farmer burst into tears, and begged so sorrowfully to be forgiven for his fault that the little man at last pitied him and said that he would speak to his lord. "I will come again at the hour of sunset three days hence and bring thee my lord's behest."

When the time came on the third day, the sprite was awaiting the farmer at the appointed spot. "The King's word," he said, "cannot be recalled, and vengeance must come. Still, since thou repentest thee of thy fault and art anxious to atone it, the curse shall not fall in thy time nor in that of thy sons, but will await thy distant posterity."

This promise comforted the farmer. The dark-green circles of grass grew again, the gay elves danced in them, and the sounds of music gladdened the fields as of old. The dread voice came at times, repeating the threat,

Daw dial,	Vengeance will come,

but the farmer passed away in peaceful old age, and his sons followed him to the churchyard without feeling any effects of the curse pronounced by the King of the fairies.

More than a hundred years after the first warning had been uttered, Madoc, the heir of Pantannas, was betrothed to Teleri, the daughter of the squire of Pen Craig Daf, and the wedding was to take place in a few weeks. It was Christmas-tide, and they made a feast at Pantannas to which Teleri and all her kin were bidden.

The feast sped merrily, and all were seated round the hearth, passing the hours with tale and song. Suddenly, above the noise of the river which flowed outside the house, they seemed to hear a voice saying:

Daeth amser ymddial.	The time for revenge is come.

A silence fell on the joyous company. They went out and listened if they could hear the voice a second time; but long though they lingered, they could make out no sound except the angry noise of the full river plunging down its rocky bed. They went back into the house; gradually their fears were chased away, and all was as before.

Again, above the sounds of mirth and the noise of the waters as they boiled over the boulders was heard a clear voice:

Daeth yr amser.	The time is come.

A dread noise crashed around them, and the house shook to its foundations. As they sat speechless with fear, behold, a shapeless hag appeared at the window. Then one, bolder than the rest, said, "What dost thou, ugly little thing, want here?"

"I have naught to do with thee, chatterer," said the hag. "I had come to tell the doom which awaits this house and that other which hopes to be allied with it, but as thou hast insulted me, the veil which conceals it shall not be lifted by me." With that she vanished, no one knew how or whither.

When she had gone, the voice proclaimed again, more loudly than before:

Daeth amser ymddial. The time for vengeance is come.

Terror and gloom fell upon all. The guests before long parted and went trembling home, and Madoc took his betrothed back to Pen Craig Daf, doing all that a fond lover could to dispel her fears, for she had been struck to the heart with nameless dread.

The hours of darkness succeeded one another wearily, and no Madoc returned to Pantannas. Morning came, but still no Madoc; and his aged parents, already shaken by the vision of the hag and the strange voices which had interrupted their joyous feast, were almost beside themselves with anxiety. As the day wore on, without any sign of Madoc, they sent messengers in all directions to seek news of him, but all they could discover was that he had turned his footsteps homewards after bidding farewell to his betrothed at Pen Craig Daf. All the countryside turned out to find him. With minute care they searched every hill and dale for many miles around, and dragged the depths of every river, but never a trace of him could they find.

When many weeks of unavailing search had gone by the father and mother sought an aged hermit who dwelt in a cave high up the country, and asked him when their lost son would come back to them. He told the lamenting parents that the judgment threatened in olden times by the fairies had overtaken the hapless youth, and bade them hope no more to see him, whether he were alive or dead. It might perhaps come to pass that after generations had gone by he would reappear, but not in their lifetime.

Time rolled on, weeks grew into months and months into years, and gradually all came to believe that the hermit had spoken true. All, that is to say, except one. The gentle maiden, Teleri, never ceased to believe that her beloved was alive and would come again. Every morning when the sun burst open the gates of dawn, she would stand upon the summit of a high rock, looking over the landscape far and near. At even, again, she would be seen at the same spot, seeking some sign of her lover's return until the sun sank behind the battlements of the west. Madoc's father and mother died, and their mortal remains were laid to rest, but Teleri never failed of hope. Year after year she watched until her bright eyes became dim and her chestnut hair was silvered. Worn out with fruitless longing, she died before her time, and they buried her in the graveyard of the old Chapel of the Fan. One by one those who had known Madoc died, and his strange disappearance became only a faint tradition.

Teleri's undying belief that her lover was still alive was, however, true. This is what had happened to him. As he was returning home from Pen Craig Daf, the sounds of the sweetest music he had ever heard in his life came out of a cave in the Raven's Rift, and he stopped to listen. The strains after a while seemed to recede further into the cave, and he stepped inside to hear better. The melody retreated further and further, and Madoc, forgetting everything else, followed it further and further into the recesses of the cavern. After he had been listening for an hour or two, as he thought, the music ceased, and suddenly remembering that after the strange events of the night his parents would be anxious for his return, he retraced his footsteps rapidly to the mouth of the cave. When he issued forth from the hollow, the sun was high in the heavens, and he realised that he had been listening to the music longer than he had at first thought. He hastened towards Pantannas, opened the door and went in. Sitting by the fire was an aged man who asked him, "Who art thou that comest in so boldly?"

A sense of bewilderment came over Madoc. He looked round him. The inside of the house seemed different from what he had been accustomed to. He went to the window and looked out. There appeared to him to be several curious differences in the aspect of the country also. He became dimly conscious that some great change had passed over his life, and answered faintly, "I am Madoc."

"Madoc?" said the aged man. "Madoc? I know thee not. There is no Madoc living in this place, nor have I ever known any man of that name. The only Madoc I have ever heard of was one who, my grandfather said, disappeared suddenly from this place, nobody knew whither, many scores of years ago."

Madoc sank on a chair and wept. The old man's heart went out to him in his grief, and he rose to comfort him. He put his hand on his shoulder, when lo! the weeping figure crumbled into thin dust.

The Drowning of the Bottom Hundred

I

IN the beginning of the sixth century, Gwyddno Garanhir was King of Ceredigion. The most valuable portion of his dominions was the great plain of the Bottom Hundred, a vast tract of level land, stretching along that part of the sea coast which now belongs to the counties of Merioneth and Cardigan. This district was populous and fertile. It contained sixteen fortified towns, superior to all the towns and cities of the Cymry excepting Caer Lleon upon Usk. It contained also one of the three privileged ports of the Isle of Britain which was called the Port of Gwyddno, and had been known to the Phœnicians and Carthaginians when they visited the island for metal in the dim dawn of history.

This lowland country was below the level of the sea, and the people of the Bottom Hundred had in very early times built an embankment of massy stone to protect it from the encroachment of that hungry element. This stony rampart had withstood the shock of the waves for centuries when Gwyddno began his reign. Watch-towers were erected along the embankment, and watchmen were appointed to guard against the first approaches of damage or decay. The whole of these towers and their companies of guards were ruled by a central castle, which commanded the seaport already mentioned, and wherein dwelt Prince Seithenyn, the son of Seithyn Saidi, who held the office of Lord High Commissioner of the Royal Embankment. Now,

Seithenyn was one of the three immortal drunkards of the Isle of Britain. He left the embankment to his deputies, who left it to their assistants, who left it to itself.

One only was there who did his duty. He was Teithrin, the son of Tathral, who had the charge of a watch-tower where the embankment ended at the point of Mochras, in the high land of Ardudwy. Teithrin kept his portion of the embankment in good condition, and paced with daily care the limits of his charge. One day he happened to stray beyond them, and observed signs of neglect that filled him with dismay. This induced him to proceed till his wanderings brought him to the embankment's southern end, in the high land of Ceredigion. He met with abundant hospitality at the towers of his colleagues and at the castle of Seithenyn: he was supposed to be walking for his amusement. He was asked no questions, and he carefully abstained from asking any. He examined and observed in silence, and when he had completed his observations he hastened to Gwyddno's palace. It had been built of choice slate stone on the rocky banks of the Mawddach, just above the point where it entered the plain of the Bottom Hundred, and in it, among green woods and sparkling waters, Garanhir lived in festal munificence. On his arrival, he was informed by the porter that the knife was in the meat, and the drink in the horn; there was revelry in the great hall, and none might enter therein but the son of a king of a privileged country or a craftsman bringing his craft. The feast was to last so many days that Teithrin despaired of delivering his message, and went in search of the King's son, Elphin.

The young Prince was fishing in the Mawddach at a spot where the river, having quitted its native mountains and not yet entered the plain, ran in alternate streams and pools sparkling through a pastoral valley. He sat under an ancient ash, enjoying the calm brightness of an autumnal noon and the melody and beauty of the flying stream on which the shifting sunbeams fell chequering through the leaves. The monotonous music of the river and the profound stillness of the air had all but sent Elphin to sleep. He was startled into attention by a sudden rush of the wind through the trees, and he heard, or seemed to hear, in the gust that hurried by him the words, "Beware of the oppression of Gwenhudiw!" The gust was momentary: the leaves ceased to rustle and the deep silence of nature returned.

Now, Gwenhudiw is the mermaid Shepherdess of Ocean: the waves are her sheep, and each ninth wave, which is always greater than the rest, is called her ram.

It was not the first time that the kingly house of Ceredigion had been warned against her oppression. Gwyddno had often heard the same mysterious words borne on the breeze. They had so haunted his memory and imagination that he had ceased to go down to the sea in ships, and dwelt inland, avoiding as far as he might the sight of the great waters. Elphin, too, had heard the prophecy before, but it had formed no part of his recent meditation. He could not, however, persuade himself that the words had not been actually spoken near him. He emerged from the shade of the trees that fringed the river, and looked round him from the rocky bank.

At this moment Teithrin discovered and approached him. Elphin knew him not and inquired his name.

"I am called," he answered, "Teithrin, the son of Tathral."

"And what seek you here?" said Elphin.

"I seek," answered Teithrin, "the Prince of the Bottom Hundred, Elphin, the son of Gwyddno Garanhir."

"You spoke," said Elphin, "as you approached?"

"Nay," said Teithrin, "I spoke never a word."

"Assuredly you did," said Elphin, "you repeated the words, 'Beware of the oppression of Gwenhudiw!'"

Teithrin again denied having spoken the words; but their mysterious impression made Elphin listen readily to his information about the decay of the royal embankment: and after their talk the Prince determined to accompany Teithrin on a visit of remonstrance to the Lord High Commissioner.

They crossed the centre of the enclosed country to the privileged Port of Gwyddno, near which stood the castle of Seithenyn. They walked towards the castle along a portion of the embankment, and Teithrin pointed out to the Prince its decayed condition.

The sea shone with the glory of the setting sun: the air was calm: and the white surf, tinged with the crimson of sunset, broke lightly on the sands below. Elphin turned his eyes from the dazzling splendour of the ocean to the green meadows of the plain: the trees that in the distance thickened into woods: the wreaths of smoke rising from among them, marking the solitary cottages or the populous towns: the massy barrier of mountains beyond, with the forest rising from their base: the precipices frowning over the forest: and the clouds resting on their summits reddened with the reflection of the west. Elphin gazed earnestly on the peopled plain, reposing in the calm of evening between the mountains and the sea, and thought with deep feelings of secret pain, how much of life and human happiness was entrusted to the ruinous mound on which he stood.

II

The sun had sunk beneath the waves when they reached the castle of Seithenyn. The sound of the harp and the song saluted them as they approached it. As they entered the great hall, which was already blazing with torchlight, they found the whole household roaring the praises of the blue buffalo horn:

Fill high the blue horn, the blue buffalo horn:
Fill high the long silver-rimmed buffalo horn:
While the roof of the hall by our chorus is torn,
Fill, fill to the brim the deep silver-rimmed horn.

Elphin and Teithrin stood some time on the floor of the hall before they attracted the attention of Seithenyn, who during the chorus was tossing and flourishing his golden goblet. The chorus had scarcely ended when he noticed them, and immediately shouted aloud, "You are welcome all four."

Elphin answered, "We thank you, we are but two."

"Two or four," said Seithenyn, "all is one. You are welcome all. When a stranger enters, the custom in other places is to begin by washing his feet. My custom is to begin by washing his throat. Seithenyn, the son of Seithyn Saidi, bids you welcome."

Elphin answered, "Elphin, the son of Gwyddno Garanhir, thanks you."

Seithenyn started up when he realised that he was in the presence of the son of the King, and with a bow intended to be gracious, invited the Prince to take his seat on his right hand. Teithrin remained at the end of the hall, on which Seithenyn shouted to him, "Come on, man, come on, sit and drink," and motioned him to seat himself next to Elphin.

"Prince Seithenyn," said Elphin, "I have visited you on a subject of deep moment. Reports have been brought to me that the embankment which has so long been entrusted to your care is in a state of dangerous decay."

"Decay," said Seithenyn, "is one thing and danger is another. Everything that is old must decay. That the embankment is old, I am free to confess; that it is somewhat rotten in parts, I will not altogether deny; that it is any the worse for that, I do most sturdily gainsay. It does its business well: it keeps out the water from the land. Cupbearer, fill."

"The stonework," said Teithrin, "is sapped and mined: the piles are rotten, broken and out of their places: the floodgates and sluices are leaky and creaky."

"Our ancestors were wiser than we," said Seithenyn; "they built the embankment in their wisdom: and if we should be so rash as to try to mend it, we should only mar it. This immortal work has stood for centuries and will stand for centuries more, if we let it alone. It is well: it works well: let well alone. Cupbearer, fill."

Elphin and Teithrin tried to reason with him, but all their words were met with the assurance that all was well with the embankment, and as every speech of the Lord High Commissioner ended with the command, "Cupbearer, fill," it was not long before he fell on sleep. The members of his household had been imitating the example of their chief, and the words of host and visitors had been punctuated by the heavy falls from their benches of men sent to sleep by the yellow mead. By the time their chief fell all except the cupbearers were lying flat on the floor.

Elphin and Teithrin were gazing in disgust upon this scene of drunken disorder, when a side door, at the upper end of the hall, to the left of Seithenyn's chair, opened, and a beautiful young girl entered the hall with her domestic bard and her attendant maidens.

It was Angharad, the daughter of Seithenyn. She gracefully

saluted Prince Elphin, and he looked with delight at the beautiful lady, whose gentle and serious loveliness contrasted so strikingly with the fallen heroes of revelry that lay scattered at her feet.

"Stranger," she said, "this seems an unfitting place for you: let me conduct you where you will be more agreeably lodged."

"Still less should I deem it fitting for you, fair maiden," said Elphin.

She answered, "The pleasure of her father is the duty of Angharad."

Elphin paused to think what he should say in reply to this, and Angharad stood still, expecting that he would follow. In this interval of silence, there came a loud gust of wind blustering through the holes of the walls. "It bids fair to be a stormy night," said Elphin.

"We are used to storms," answered Angharad. "We are far from the mountains, between the lowlands and the sea, and the winds blow round us from all quarters."

There was another pause of deep silence; then there came another gust of wind, pealing like thunder through the holes. Amidst the fallen and sleeping revellers, the confused and littered hall, the low and wavering torches, Angharad, lovely always, shone with single and surpassing loveliness. The gust died away in murmurs and swelled again into thunder and died away in murmurs again: and, as it died away, mixed with the murmurs of ocean, a voice, that seemed one of the many voices of the wind, pronounced the ominous words, "Beware of the oppression of Gwenhudiw!"

They looked at each other, as if questioning whether all had heard alike.

"Did you not hear a voice?" said Angharad, after a pause.

"The same," said Elphin, "which has before seemed to say to me, 'Beware of the oppression of Gwenhudiw!'"

Teithrin hurried forth on the rampart: Angharad turned pale and leaned against a pillar of the hall. Elphin was amazed and awed, absorbed as his feelings were in her. The sleepers on the floor made an uneasy movement and uttered a cry.

Teithrin returned. "What saw you?" said Elphin.

Teithrin answered, "A tempest is coming from the west. The

moon has waned three days, and is half hidden in clouds, just visible above the mountains: the bank of clouds is black in the west: the scud is flying before them: and the white waves are rolling to the shore."

"This is the highest of the spring tides," said Angharad, "and they are very terrible in the storms from the west when the spray flies over the embankment and the breakers shake the tower which has its foot in the surf."

"Whence was the voice," said Elphin, "which we heard erewhile? Was it the cry of a sleeper in his drink, or an error of the fancy, or a warning voice from the elements?"

"It was surely nothing earthly," said Angharad, "nor was it an error of the fancy, for we all heard the words, 'Beware of the oppression of Gwenhudiw!' Often and often in the storms of the spring tides have I feared to see her roll her power over the fields of the Bottom Hundred."

"Pray Heaven she do not to-night," said Teithrin.

"Can there be such a danger?" said Elphin.

"I think," said Teithrin, "of the decay I have seen, and I fear the voice I have heard."

A long pause of deep silence ensued, during which they heard the peals of the wind, and the increasing sound of the rising sea, swelling ever into wilder and more menacing tumult, till, with one terrific impulse, the whole violence of the tempest seemed to burst upon the shore. Before long there came a tremendous crash. The tower, which had its foot in the sea, had long been sapped by the waves: and the storm hurled it into the surf, carrying with it a portion of the wall of the main building, and revealing through the chasm the white raging of the breakers beneath the blackness of the midnight storm. The wind rushed into the hall, putting out the torches within the line of its course, tossing the grey locks and loose mantle of the bard and the light white drapery and long black tresses of Angharad. With the crash of the falling tower, and the shrieks of the women the sleepers started from the floor, staring with drunken amazement, and Seithenyn rose staggering from his chair.

The Lord High Commissioner of the Royal Embankment leaned against a pillar and stared at the sea through the rifted wall with wild and vacant surprise. Then he looked at Elphin and Teithrin, at his daughter and at the members of his household, but the longer he looked, the less clearly he saw: and the longer he pondered, the less he understood. He felt the rush of the wind: he saw the white foam of the sea: his ears were dizzy with their mingled roar. He remained at length motionless, leaning against the pillar, and gazing on the breakers with fixed and glaring vacancy.

"The sleepers of the Bottom Hundred," said Elphin, "they who sleep in peace and security, trusting to the vigilance of Seithenyn, what will become of them?"

"Warn them with the beacon fire," said Teithrin, "if there be fuel on the summit of the landward tower."

"That, of course, has been neglected too," said Elphin.

"Not so," said Angharad, "that has been my charge."

Teithrin seized a torch and ascended the eastern tower, and in a few minutes the party in the hall beheld the breakers reddening with the reflected fire, and deeper and yet deeper crimson tinging the whirling foam and sheeting the massy darkness of the bursting waves.

An unusual tumult mingled with the roar of the waves. Teithrin rushed into the hall, exclaiming, "All is over! The mound is broken and the spring tide is rolling through the breach."

Another portion of the castle wall fell into the mining waves, and by the dim and thickly-clouded moonlight, and the red blaze of the beacon fire, they beheld a torrent pouring in from the sea upon the plain and rushing immediately beneath the castle walls, which, as well as the points of the embankment that formed the sides of the breach, continued to crumble away into the waters.

"Who has done this?" shouted Seithenyn. "Show me the enemy."

"There is no enemy but the sea," said Elphin, "to which you, in your drunken madness, have abandoned the land. Think, if you can think, of what is passing in the plain. The storm drowns the cries of your victims, but the curses of the perishing are upon you."

"Show me the enemy," shouted Seithenyn, drawing his sword furiously and flourishing it over his head.

"There is no enemy but the sea," said Elphin, "against which your sword avails not."

"Who dares to say so?" said Seithenyn. "Who dares to say that there is an enemy on earth against whom the sword of Seithenyn is unavailing? Thus, thus I prove the falsehood." And springing suddenly forward, he leaped into the torrent, flourishing his sword as he descended.

"Oh, my unhappy father!" sobbed Angharad, veiling her face with her arm on the shoulder of one of her female attendants.

"We must quit the castle," said Teithrin, "or we shall be buried in its ruins. We have but one path of safety, along the summit of the embankment, if there be not another breach between us and the high land, and if we can keep our footing in this storm. But let us go: the walls are melting away like snow."

Angharad, recovering from the first shock of Seithenyn's catastrophe, became awake to the imminent danger. The spirit of the Cymric female, vigilant and energetic in peril, disposed her and her attendant maidens to use their best exertions for their own preservation. Following the advice and example of Elphin and Teithrin, they armed themselves with spears, which they took down from the walls.

Teithrin led the way, striking the point of his spear firmly into the earth and leaning from it on the wind. Angharad followed in the same manner: Elphin followed Angharad; the attendant maidens followed Elphin: and the bard followed the female train. Behind them went the cupbearers, and behind them reeled those who were able and willing to move.

In front of them, as they marched, was the volumed blackness of the storm: the breakers burst white in the faint and scarcely perceptible moonlight: within the mound the waters rushed and rose: the red light of the beacon fire fell on them from behind: the surf rolled up the side of the embankment and broke almost at their feet: the spray flew above their heads, and it was only by thrusting their spears into the stony ground that they bore themselves up against the wind.

They had not proceeded far when the tide began to recede,

the wind to abate somewhat of its violence, and the moon to look on them at intervals through the rifted clouds, disclosing the desolation of the flooded plain, silvering the angry surf, gleaming on the distant mountains and revealing a lengthened prospect of their solitary path that lay in its irregular line like a ribbon on the deep. Morning dawned before they reached safety; daylight showed fully how dreadful was the destruction. The foaming waves were covering the fertile plains which had been the habitation and support of a flourishing population. Of the inhabitants, only the party led by Teithrin from Seithenyn's castle and a few who saw the beacon fire in time to run to the high lands of Ardudwy and Eryri escaped destruction.

The nearest town to the submerged realm of Gwyddno is Aberdovey. If you stand on the beach there, you will sometimes hear in the long twilight evening chimes and peals of bells, sometimes near, sometimes distant, sounding low and sweet like a call to prayer, or as rejoicing for a victory. The sounds come from the bells of one of Gwyddno's drowned churches, and these are "The Bells of Aberdovey" that the song speaks about.

Elidyr's Sojourn in Fairy-Land

IN that country of crosses, ruined chapels and rocking stones, caers and tumuli, cromlechs and camps, which is sometimes known as Dewisland, there once lived a boy named Elidyr whose father and mother wished him to become a priest. They accordingly sent him every day to the monks of St. David's to learn his letters, but the little rascal much preferred hoop and ball to book-learning; all that went in at one ear came out at the other, and as a scholar he therefore left much to be desired. His teachers, remembering that Solomon had said, "He that spareth his rod hateth his son, but he that loveth him chasteneth him betimes," showed their affection towards their pupil in the manner he advised. At first they corrected him lightly and infrequently, but Elidyr did not amend his ways, and before long not a lesson passed without chastisement. Not only were the stripes more frequent, but they also became more severe, till Elidyr could stand them no longer. So one day when he was twelve years old he ran away: he went on and on, and the further he got the happier he felt. Knowing that a search would be made for him, he looked diligently for a hiding place, but for a long time he could find no place where he could feel safe. At last he came to a river: under the hollow bank of this, there was a beautiful hiding place, where no pursuer would ever expect to find a runaway. Into this he crept and slept that night as soundly as the best little boy who ever tired himself out with lessons. The next day he realised that, glorious as his hiding place was as an escape from books and thwackings, it had its disadvantages: the chief was that there was nothing to eat and drink, and that is a very serious thing for a growing boy with a healthy appetite. It was not safe to go out even to look for hips and haws, because when he lifted his head above the river bank he saw men and women searching all over the countryside for him. He became hungrier and hungrier, and oh, how slowly the time passed! It was the longest day Elidyr had ever known: the sun simply crawled across the heavens, and it seemed to be an age before it dipped its red rim in the waters of St. Bride's Bay. He was no better off even when the sun did set, because night is worse than day when you cannot sleep, and it is very difficult to get even forty winks when you have an aching void inside you. Every time he woke up he felt hungrier, and he made up his mind to return home as soon as it was light enough for him to find his way.

Better two thrashings—for he knew that his father would lay on as well as the monks—than the wolf which was tearing his inside. When the shades of night were disappearing, he got up to start off, when to his intense surprise two little pigmies appeared to him and said, "Come with us, and we will lead you to a land full of sports and delights." Very curiously his hunger vanished that very minute, and with the hunger vanished the desire to return to those hateful lessons and thrashings. So he upped with him and offed with him with the two pigmies. They went first through an underground passage all in the dark, but soon they came out into a most beautiful country. There were purling streams, lush meadows and wooded hills, all as pleasant as can be.

The two little men led Elidyr to a magnificent palace. "What is this place?" asked the truant. "This is the palace of the King of Faery," answered his guides. They took him in, and there they found the King sitting on a splendid throne, with his courtiers in magnificent dresses all about him. He asked Elidyr who he was and whence he came. Elidyr told him, and the King said, "Thou shalt attend my son." The King then waved him away, and the King's son, who was about the same age as Elidyr, took him out of the court.

Then began a time of supreme happiness to Elidyr. He waited on the King's son and joined in all the games and sports of the little men. They were little, but they were not mis-shapen dwarfs, for all their limbs were well-proportioned.

They were fair of complexion, and their hair was thick and

long, falling over their shoulders like that of women. They rode little horses about the size of greyhounds, and they never ate flesh nor fish, but lived on messes of milk flavoured with saffron. They took no oaths, but never spoke a lie, for there was nothing they detested so much as falsehood. They scoffed at men for their struggles, follies, vanities, fickleness, treacheries and lies. But they worshipped none, unless you might say they were worshippers of Truth. The country in which they lived was beautiful, as has already been described, but there was this that was curious about it. The sun never shone and clouds were always over the sky, so that even the days were obscure and the nights were pitch dark, for neither moon nor stars ever gave any light.

After a time Elidyr began to long for his mother, and he begged to be allowed to go and visit his old home. The King gave him permission, and the two little men who had brought him to the realm of Faery led him through the underground passage to the upper earth, and right up to his mother's cottage, keeping him invisible to all on the way. Imagine his mother's joy when he entered, for she had thought he was lost for ever. She plied him with questions and he had to tell her everything about himself and the bourne from which he had returned. She begged him to stay with her, but he had given his word to go back, and soon he departed, after making his mother promise not to tell where he was or with whom. After this he often went to visit his mother, sometimes by the road by which he had first returned, sometimes by others. At first he was not allowed to go alone, but inasmuch as he always kept his promise to come back, he was subsequently permitted to go by himself.

Now one day when Elidyr was with his mother, he told her of the heavy yellow balls which the King's son and he used in their play. His mother knew that they must be made of gold, and she said to him, "Bring one of them with you next time you come." "It would not be right to do that," said the boy. "What is the harm?" asked his mother. "I have been told never to bring anything with me to earth," replied Elidyr. "Surely, out of the hundreds of balls which the King's son has, he would not miss just one," pleaded the mother, and the boy reluctantly consented. Some days after, when he thought no one was looking, he took up one of the golden balls, and started off to his mother's cottage, walking at first slowly, but increasing his pace as he drew nearer to the upper air. Just as he emerged out of the underground passage on to the earth, he thought he heard tiny footsteps pattering behind him, and he started to run. Turning his head round, he saw two little men running after him and looking very grim. He put his best foot forward and tore ahead; the little men raced after him, but Elidyr having the start reached the cottage first. When he reached the threshold, he stumbled and fell, and the golden ball rolled out of his hand right to the feet of his mother. At that moment the two little men jumped over him as he lay sprawling, seized the ball and rushed out of the house. As they passed Elidyr they spat at him and shouted, "Thief, traitor, false mortal," and other terms of reproach.

Full of grief and shame, he went sadly back to the river bank where the underground passage commenced, determined to go back to the land of the little men to tell them how sorry he was that he had listened to his mother's evil counsel, but he could find no trace of any opening. Again and again he searched, but never could he find any way back to that fair country. So after a time he went back to the monastery, and tried to deaden his longing for fairy land by devotion to learning. In due time he became a monk. The story of his sojourn in Fairy-land gradually leaked out, and men used to come and ask him about the land of the little men, but he could never speak of the happy time he had spent there without shedding tears.

Now it happened that when Elidyr was old, David, the second Bishop of St. David's, came to visit the monastery and ask him about the manners and customs of the little men. Above all, he was curious to know what language they spoke, and Elidyr told him some of their words. When they asked for water they would say, "Udor udorum," and when they wanted salt, they said, "Halgei udorum." Now the Bishop knew that the Greek for water is ὕδωρ and for salt ἅλζ, and he thus discovered that the language of the fairies greatly resembles that of the ancient Greeks.

Rhys and Llywelyn

TWO farm servants named Rhys and Llywelyn were one fine evening at twilight returning home to Llwyn y Ffynon from the mountain, where they had been cutting peat. They were walking through a wood when Rhys suddenly said, "Stop: listen to that enchanting music: that's a tune I've danced to a hundred times and I can't resist it now. I must find the musicians and have my dance: if you don't want to stop, you can go and have your supper and I'll be with you presently."

"Music and dancing indeed," replied Llywelyn, "I hear no music and how should you? Come, come, no nonsense, come home with me."

He might have spared his breath to cool the porridge which was awaiting him at Llwyn y Ffynon, for Rhys plunged into the trees, leaving Llywelyn to pursue his homeward journey alone. As he was walking along, he thought that all Rhys's talk about music must have been just an excuse for going to the alehouse, which was five miles away; so he ate his supper and retired to rest in the stable loft without any anxiety about his companion. Nor was he troubled about him when he woke up in the middle of the night and found himself alone, reflecting that under the influence of the ale Rhys would probably go a-wooing and return before morning as he had often done before.

When morning came, however, there was no Rhys, and when questioned by his master, Llywelyn said that he had gone off suddenly the night before, presumably to the alehouse. As there was a heavy day's work to be gone through, a messenger was sent to the alehouse to inquire about Rhys, but came back with the information that Rhys had not been there at all. By-and-by, his master thought it advisable to question Llywelyn more closely as to where, how and why Rhys had left him. Llywelyn stated that as they were walking through the wood, Rhys had suddenly heard music and left him, as he said, to join the dance.

"Did you hear the music?" inquired his master, and when Llywelyn replied that he had not, his account of his fellow-servant's disappearance was considered very unsatisfactory.

A search was made for the lost Rhys, but not a trace of him could be found. There had been no dance in the whole country round: not a sound of music had reached the ear of anyone: and suspicion gradually fell on Llywelyn. It was supposed that he must have quarrelled with Rhys on the way home and murdered him, and he was arrested and put in prison. He protested his innocence, but as he could give no account of his companion's disappearance except that, at the sound of music which no one had heard, he had suddenly gone off to a dance which had not taken place, he was generally thought to be guilty, and he was kept in prison until the dead body could be found and his guilt could be brought home to him.

Things remained thus for nearly a year, when a newcomer into the neighbourhood, who had some experience of fairy ways and customs, suggested that he and a company of neighbours should go with Llywelyn to the place where he had parted from Rhys. This was agreed to and they came to a fairy ring.

"This is the very spot," said Llywelyn, "and hush, I hear music; melodious harps I hear."

The whole company listened, but could hear nothing, and told Llywelyn so.

"Put your foot on mine, David," said Llywelyn, whose foot was now upon the outward edge of the fairy circle, to one of the company. David put his foot on Llywelyn's, and so did they all, one after another: and then they heard the sound of many harps in full concert, and saw within the circle a number of little figures enjoying themselves vastly. They were dancing round and round the ring with hands joined, and among them was Rhys, footing it with the best of them.

As he came whirling by, Llywelyn seized hold of his smock frock and switched him out of the circle, taking great care not to overstep the edge of the ring.

"Let me finish my dance," said Rhys, "I never enjoyed a dance like this before, and I have not been above five minutes at it. Let me return to the dance."

"Five minutes, indeed," said the enraged Llywelyn, "you've been there long enough to come near getting me hanged, anyhow. I've been accused of murdering you, and you must clear my character. Come, answer for yourself and account for your conduct." And he restrained him by main force.

But to all the questions with which he was plied, he could only reply that he had been dancing for about five minutes. Of the people with whom he was, he could give no account whatever, except that they danced exquisitely. They were strangers to him, he said. He had not eaten or drunk or slept, and he was in the same clothes as when he disappeared. He became sad, sullen and silent, took to his bed and before long died.

Lowri Dafydd Earns a Purse of Gold

LOWRI DAFYDD had just arrived at Hafodydd Brithion to nurse a sick woman, when a fine-looking man galloped up to the door on a noble grey horse and said in a loud voice, "Is Lowri Dafydd here?"

"Yes, sir," answered Lowri in a very meek voice.

"Then come with me at once," said the fine-looking man.

"But I have my duty to do here," remonstrated Lowri.

"Come with me at once," repeated the fine-looking man; and he spoke in such a tone that Lowri had not the courage to say no.

She mounted behind him, and off they went, like the flight of a swallow, through Cwmllan, down Nant yr Aran, and over the Gader to Cwm Hafod Ruffydd, before the poor woman had time even to say "Oh!"

When they reached Cwm Hafod Ruffydd, Lowri saw a magnificent mansion before her, splendidly lit up with such lamps as she had never seen before. They entered the court, and a crowd of servants in gorgeous liveries came to meet them.

"Lead her to the bed-chamber," said the fine-looking man; and Lowri was conducted through the great hall into a bed-chamber which surpassed in luxury and splendour anything she had ever dreamed of, let alone seen. There the mistress of the house, to whose aid she had been summoned, was awaiting her.

Lowri nursed her with her accustomed skill, and stayed with

her until the lady was completely recovered. It was the pleasantest episode of Lowri's life; there was festivity day and night; dancing, singing and merriment went on ceaselessly. She was very sad when the time came for her to depart. The fine-looking man gave her a great, heavy purse, with the order not to open it until she reached her own house. Then he bade one of his servants escort her back the same way that she had come. When she reached home she opened the purse, and to her intense delight it was full of gold. She lived happily on these earnings to the end of her life.

The Llanfabon Changeling

AT a farmhouse called Berth Gron, in the parish of Llanfabon, there once lived a young widow. She had a little boy whom she loved more than her own eyes. He was her only comfort, and she was afraid of letting the sun shine on him, as the saying goes. Pryderi—that was the name she had given him—was about three years old, and a fine child for his age.

At this time the parish of Llanfabon was full of fairies. On nights when the moon was bright, they often used to keep the hard-working farmers awake with their music until the cock crew in the morning. On nights when the moon was dark, they delighted in luring men into desolate bogs by displaying false lights. Even in the daytime they would play tricks on people if they were not very careful.

The widow knew that the Fair Family were very fond of stealing babies out of their cradles, and you can imagine how careful she was of her little treasure. She hated leaving him out of her sight by night or day: if ever she had to do so, she was miserable until she returned to him and found him safe and sound.

One day when he was lying asleep in his cradle, she heard the cows in the byre lowing piteously as if they were in great pain. As there was nobody in the house but herself to look after her precious boy, she was afraid at first of going out to see what was amiss. The lowing, however, became more and more agonised, and she became frightened. Not being able to stand it any longer, she rushed out, forgetting in her fright to place the tongs crossways on the cradle.

When she got to the cow house, she was amazed to find that there was nothing whatever the matter with the cattle: they were chewing their cud placidly, and they turned their great meek eyes in mild surprise upon her, evidently wondering why she had burst in upon them so unceremoniously. Realising that she had been the victim of some deception, she ran back to the house as fast as her feet could carry her, and to the cradle. She was afraid of finding it empty, but bending over it she found a little boy in it who greeted her with "Mother." She looked hard at him: he was very like Pryderi, and yet there was something about him which made her think that he was different from him. At last she said doubtingly, "You are not my child."

"I am truly," said the little one. "What do you mean, mother?"

But something kept whispering to her constantly that he was not her child, and as time went on she became convinced that she was right. The little boy after a while became cross and fretful, unlike Pryderi, who was always as good as gold. In a whole year he never grew at all.

Pryderi, on the other hand, was a very growing child. Besides, the little fellow seemed to get uglier every day, whereas Pryderi had been getting prettier and prettier: at least his mother thought so. She did not know what to do.

Now, there was in the parish of Llanfabon a man who had the reputation of being well informed on matters which are dark to most people. This reputation he had gained by living at a place called the Castle of the Night. This castle had been built of stones from Llanfabon Church, and was haunted. Many men had tried to live there, but had been compelled to leave because ghosts plagued them so. That this man was able to dwell there in seeming peace and comfort was proof positive, in the eyes of the people of Llanfabon, that he had some control at least over the powers of darkness.

The widow went to this wise man and laid her trouble before him. After hearing her story he said to her, "If you follow my directions faithfully and minutely, I think I shall be able to help you. At noon to-morrow take an eggshell and prepare to brew some beer in it. See that the boy watches what you are doing, but take care not to tell him to pay attention. He will ask you what you are doing. You are to say, 'I am brewing beer for the harvestmen.' Listen carefully to what he says when he hears that, but pretend not to catch it. After you have put him to bed to-morrow night, come and tell me all about it."

The widow returned home, and the next day at noon she followed the cunning man's advice. She took an eggshell and got everything ready for brewing beer. The boy stood by her, watching her as a cat watches a mouse. Presently he asked, "What are you doing, mother?" She said, "I am brewing beer for the harvestmen, my boy." Then the boy said quietly to himself:

"I am very old this day,
I was living before my birth,
I remember yonder oak
An acorn in the earth,
But I never saw the egg of a hen
Brewing beer for harvestmen."

The widow heard what he said, but pretended not to have caught it, and asked, "What did you say, my son?" He said, "Nothing, mother." She then turned round and saw that he was very cross, and the angry expression on his face made him very repulsive to look upon.

After she had put him to bed that night, the widow went to the Castle of the Night, as she had been ordered. As soon as she entered, the wise man asked, "Were you able to catch what he said?"

"He spoke very quietly to himself," answered the widow, "but I am quite sure that what he said was:

'I am very old this day,
I was living before my birth,
I remember yonder oak
An acorn in the earth,
But I never saw the egg of a hen
Brewing beer for harvestmen.'"

"It is well," said the wise man. "If you follow my directions faithfully and minutely, I think I shall be able to help you. The moon will be full in four days, and you must go at midnight to where the four roads meet above the Ford of the Bell. Hide yourself somewhere where you can see everything that comes along any of the roads without being seen yourself. Whatever happens, do not stir or utter a sound. If you do, my plans will be frustrated and your own life will be in danger. Come to me the day after and tell me what you see."

By midnight on the appointed day the widow had concealed herself carefully behind a large bush near the cross-roads above the Ford of the Bell, where she could see everything that came along any of the four roads without being seen herself. For a long time there was nothing to be seen or heard: the moon shone brightly, and the melancholy silence of midnight lay over all. Before long dark clouds obscured the moon, and at last the anxious widow heard the faint sounds of music in the far distance. The strains came nearer and nearer, and she listened with rapt attention. Before long the melody was close at hand, and she saw a procession of fairies coming along one of the roads. Soon the vanguard of the procession came up, and she saw that there were hundreds of fairies marching along. They were singing the sweetest songs she had ever heard, and she felt that she could listen to them for ever. Just as the middle of the procession came opposite her hiding place, the moon emerged from behind a black cloud, and in the clear, cold light which then flooded the earth she beheld a sight which turned her pleasure into bitter pain and made her heart beat almost out of her body. Walking between two fairies was her own dear little boy. She nearly forgot herself altogether, and was on the point of springing into the midst of the fairies to snatch her darling from them. But she remembered in time that the wise man had warned her that his plans would be upset and her own life in danger if she carried out her intention, and controlling herself by a supreme effort she neither stirred nor uttered a sound. When the long procession had wound itself past and the music had died away in the distance, she issued from her concealment and went home to bed, but her heart was so full of longing for her lost child that she never slept a wink all night.

On the morrow she went to the wise man early. He was

expecting her, and as she entered he perceived by her looks that she had seen something to disturb her. She told him what she had witnessed at the cross-roads, and he again said, 'It is well. If you will follow my directions faithfully and minutely, I think I shall be able to help you."

He then brought out a great book, bound in calf-skin, opened it, and pored long over it. After much deliberation he said, "You must find a black hen without a single white feather, or one of any other colour than black. Do you burn peat or wood?"

"I burn peat," said the widow.

"After you have found the hen," resumed the wise man, "you must light a wood fire and bake the hen before it, with its feathers and all intact. After you have placed it to bake before the fire, close every passage and hole in the wall, leaving only the chimney open. After that, avoid looking at the boy, but watch the hen baking, and do not take your eyes off it until the last feather has fallen off it."

Strange as the directions of the wise man appeared, she determined to follow them as faithfully and minutely as she had the previous directions. But oh, the weary tramp she had before she could find a black hen without a single white feather or one of any other colour than black. She tried every farm in the parish of Llanfabon in vain, and she was nearly driven to the conclusion that if this breed of hens had ever existed on the earth it had become extinct. It was weeks before she secured the right hen, and it was at a farm miles away from Llanfabon that she was successful in her search.

Her repeated disappointments were all the more bitter because she was forced to hide her disgust with the little fellow who was there instead of her boy. When he addressed her as "Mother," it was almost more than she could bear, but she was just able to make no difference in her behaviour towards him, though he seemed to be getting smaller, crosser and uglier every day.

Having found the black hen, she built up a wood fire, and when it was burning brightly she wrung the hen's neck and placed it as it was, feathers and all, in front of the fire. She then closed every passage and hole in the walls, leaving only the chimney open, and sat in front of the fire to watch the hen baking. The little fellow called to her several times, but though she answered him she was careful not to look at him. After a bit she fell into a swoon. When she came out of it she saw that all the feathers had fallen off the hen, and looking round the house she saw that the changeling had disappeared. Then she heard the strains of music outside the house, and they were the same as those she had heard at the cross-roads. All of a sudden the music ceased, and she heard a little boy's voice calling, "Mother." She rushed out, and lo! and behold, who should be standing within a few paces of the threshold but her own dear little boy. She snatched him up in her arms and almost smothered him with kisses. She laughed and wept in turn, and her joy was greater than words can tell. When asked where he had been all this long while, the little boy had no account to give of himself except that he had been listening to lovely music. He was pale and wan and thin, but under his mother's loving care he soon became his bonny self again, and mother and son lived happily ever afterwards.

Why the Red Dragon Is the Emblem of Wales

AFTER the Treachery of the Long Knives, King Vortigern called together his twelve wise men and asked them what he should do. They said to him: "Retire to the remote boundaries of your kingdom, and there build and fortify a city to defend yourself. The Saxon people you have received are treacherous, and they are seeking to subdue you by guile. Even during your life they will, if they can, seize upon all the countries which are subject to your power. How much more will they attempt it after your death?"

The King was pleased with this advice, and departing with his wise men travelled through many parts of his territories in search of a convenient place for building a citadel. Far and wide they travelled, but nowhere could they find a suitable place until they came to the mountains of Eryri, in Gwynedd. On the summit of one of these, which was then called Dinas Ffaraon, they discovered a fine place to build a fortress. The wise men said to the King: "Build here a city, for in this place you will be secure against the barbarians."

Then the King sent for artificers, carpenters and stonemasons, and collected all the materials for building; in the night, however, the whole of these disappeared, and by morning nothing remained of all that had been provided. Materials were procured from all parts a second time, but a second time they disappeared in the night. A third time everything was brought together for building, but by morning again not a trace of them remained. Vortigern called his wise men together and asked them the cause of this marvel. They replied: "You must find a child born without a father, put him to death, and sprinkle with his blood the ground on which the citadel is to be built, or you will never accomplish your purpose."

This did not appear such strange advice to King Vortigern as it does to us. In olden times there were very cruel practices in connection with building. Sometimes a human victim was sacrificed in order that his blood might be used as cement; at other times a living person was walled in a new building—often an innocent little child.

The King thought the advice of his wise men was good, and sent messengers throughout Britain in search of a child born without a father. After having inquired in vain in all the provinces, they came to a field in Bassaleg, where a party of boys were playing at ball. Two of them were quarrelling, and one of them said to the other, "O boy without a father, no good will ever happen to you." The messengers concluded that this was the boy they were searching for; they had him led away and conducted him before Vortigern the King.

The next day the King, his wise men, his soldiers and retinue, his artificers, carpenters and stonemasons, assembled for the ceremony of putting the boy to death. Then the boy said to the King, "Why have your servants brought me hither?" "That you may be put to death," replied the King, "and that the ground on which my citadel is to stand may be sprinkled with your blood, without which I shall be unable to build it." "Who," said the boy, "instructed you to do this?" "My wise men," replied the King. "Order them hither," returned the boy.

This being done, he thus questioned the wise men: "By what means was it revealed to you that this citadel could not be built unless the spot were sprinkled with my blood? Speak without disguise, and declare who discovered me to you." Then turning to the King, "I will soon," said he, "unfold to you everything; but I desire to question your wise men and wish them to disclose to you what is hidden underneath this pavement." They could not do so and acknowledged their ignorance. Thereupon the boy said, "There is a pool; come and dig." They did so, and found a pool even as the boy had said. "Now," he continued, turning to the wise men again, "tell me what is in the pool." But they were ashamed and made no reply. "I," said the boy, "can discover it to you if the wise men cannot. There are two vases in the pool." They examined and found that it was so. Continuing his questions, "What is in the vases?" he asked. They were again silent. "There is a tent in them," said the boy; "separate them and you shall find it so."

This being done by the King's command, there was found in them a folded tent. The boy, going on with his questions, asked the wise men what was in it. But they knew not what to reply. "There are," said he, "two serpents, one white and one red; unfold the tent." They obeyed, and two sleeping serpents were discovered. "Consider attentively," said the boy, "what the serpents do." They began to struggle with each other, and the white one, raising himself up, threw down the other into the middle of the tent and sometimes drove him to the edge of it, and this was repeated thrice. At length the red one, apparently the weaker of the two, recovering his strength, expelled the white one from the tent, and the latter, being pursued through the pool by the red one, disappeared.

Then the boy asked the wise men what was signified by this wonderful omen, but they had again to confess their ignorance. "I will now," said he to the King, "unfold to you the meaning of this mystery. The pool is the emblem of this world, and the tent that of your kingdom; the two serpents are two dragons; the red serpent is your dragon, but the white serpent is the dragon of the Saxons, who occupy several provinces and districts of Britain, even almost from sea to sea. At length, however, our people shall rise and drive the Saxon race beyond the sea whence they have come; but do you depart from this place where you are not permitted to erect a citadel, you must seek another spot for laying your foundations."

Vortigern, perceiving the ignorance and deceit of the magicians, ordered them to be put to death, and their graves were dug in a neighbouring field. The boy's life was spared; he became known to fame afterwards as the great magician Myrddin Emrys (or Merlin, as he is called in English), and the mountain on which he proved his mighty power was called in after time Dinas Emrys instead of Dinas Ffaraon. He remained in the Dinas for a long time, until he was joined by Aurelius Ambrosius, who persuaded him to go away with him. When they were about to set out, Myrddin placed all his treasure in a golden cauldron and hid it in a cave. On the mouth of the cave he rolled a huge stone, which he covered up with earth and green turf, so that it was impossible for anyone to find it. This wealth he intended to be the property of some special person in a future generation. This heir is to be a youth with yellow hair and blue eyes, and when he comes to the Dinas a bell will ring to invite him into the cave, which will open out of its own accord as soon as his foot touches it.

Llyn Cwm Llwch

At the foot of Pen y Fan, the principal peak of the Beacons of Brecon, is a lake called Llyn Cwm Llwch, overhung by frowning precipices, the home of croaking ravens, the only birds which will venture near the dark waters of the mere.

In very ancient times there was a door in a rock hard by, which opened once in each year—on May Day—and disclosed a passage leading to a small island in the centre of the lake. This island was, however, invisible to those who stood upon the shore. Those who ventured down the secret passage on May Day were most graciously received by the fairies inhabiting the island, whose beauty was only equalled by their courtesy to their guests. They entertained them with delicious fruits and exquisite music, and disclosed to them many events of the future. They laid down one condition only, and that was that none of the produce of the island was to be carried away, because the island was sacred.

It happened upon one of these annual visits that an evil visitor, when he was about to leave the island, put a flower in his pocket. His theft did him no good: as soon as he reached unhallowed ground his senses left him, and he was a jibbering idiot all the days of his life. Of this injury the fairies took no notice at the time. They dismissed the rest of their guests with their accustomed courtesy, and the door was closed as usual. But their resentment ran high. Those who went to pay them a visit on May Day the year after failed to find the door, and it has never been found from that day to this.

Some hundreds of years after, the inhabitants of the neighbourhood formed a plan of draining the lake to see whether the fairies had left any treasure at the bottom of it. They assembled at the lake one day in considerable numbers with spades and pickaxes, and set to work with such vigour that in a few hours they had dug a trench thirty yards in depth (the remains of it may still be seen). At last they had got so near the mere that it seemed as if another blow of the pickaxe would break through the bank and let out the water. Just as this blow was going to be given, just as the pickaxe was lifted up to complete the undertaking, a flash of lightning was seen which averted the blow; the sky became black, a loud peal of thunder rolled among the mountains, waking their thousand echoes, and all the workmen ran from the trench and stood in awe upon the brink of the lake. As the sound of the thunder died away, a sort of ripple was perceived on the face of the water, and the centre of the lake became violently agitated. From this boiling eddy was seen to arise a figure of gigantic stature, whose hair and beard were at least three yards in length. Standing nearly half out of the water, he addressed the workmen:

"If you disturb my peace,
Be warned that I will drown
The valley of the Usk,
Beginning with Brecon town."

He concluded by saying, "Remember the token of the cat," and then disappeared amidst a terrific storm of thunder and lightning.

When the wonder and fear had a little subsided, the people began to discuss the matter together. They could perfectly understand the warning, but they were much perplexed about the "token of the cat," which conveyed no meaning at all to them. At this point an old man of the name of Thomas Sion Rhydderch came forward and said he could explain the words. "When I was a young lad," he said, "I was tending some sheep on yonder mountain, and a woman, who had a very troublesome cat, asked me to take it with me one morning to drown it in this lake. When I arrived here, I took off my garter and with it tied a large stone to the cat's neck, and threw it into the water. The cat of course immediately sank out of sight. The next day I went in a boat on Llyn Syfaddon to fish. What should I see floating in the middle of the lake but the very cat which I had drowned in Llyn Cwm Llwch, with my garter around its body! I was much frightened, because the two lakes are miles apart and there is no stream flowing from the one to the other, and I have never mentioned it to a living soul until to-day."

From this they concluded that there is some mysterious connection between Llyn Syfaddon and Llyn Cwm Llwch, and that, though the latter is but small, yet if they attempted to drain it, the large lake would assist its little relative and avenge any injury done to it by discharging its vast body of water over the whole of the adjacent country. Accordingly they left the trench which they had dug unfinished and departed to their homes.

The Adventures of Three Farmers

THREE men who once went to Beddgelert Fair had strange adventures before they reached home.

One of them was the farmer of the Gilwern. On his way home he came across the Fair Family dancing. He looked on for hours, and the music was so sweet that he felt certain that even in Heaven he would not hear sweeter. But he forgot himself while listening and went too near. When they noticed him the little people threw a kind of dust in his eyes, and while he was wiping it away they betook themselves somewhere out of his sight, so that he neither saw nor heard anything more of them.

This was what befell the second, the farmer of the Ffridd. He also saw a company of fairies engaged in their revels, and while he was watching them he fell asleep. As he slept they bound him so tightly that he could not have stirred, and then they covered him over with a veil of gossamer, so that nobody could see him in case he called for help. As he did not return home his family made a minute search for him, in vain. However, about the same time the following night the fairies came and liberated him, and he shortly woke up after sleeping a whole night and a day. After awaking he had no idea where on earth he was; he wandered about on the slopes of the Gader and near the Gors Fawr until the cock crew, when he found where he was, namely, less than a quarter of a mile from his home.

The third was the farmer of Drws y Coed. He was going home along the old road over the Gader, and when he was near the top he saw a fine, handsome house, in which there was a rare merrymaking. He knew very well that there was no such building anywhere on his way, and it made him think that he had mistaken his road and gone astray. He therefore resolved to turn into the house to ask for a night's lodging. His request was readily granted, and when he entered he thought that a wedding feast *(neithior)* was being celebrated, such was the jollity, the singing and the dancing. The house was full of young men and women and children, all disporting as merrily as could be. Presently the company began to disperse one by one, and he asked if he might go to bed. He was led into a beautiful bed-chamber, where there was a bed of the softest down covered with bed-clothes as white as snow. He at once undressed, went into bed, and slept quietly enough until the morning. He opened his eyes and found he was sleeping on the open bog-land, with a clump of rushes as his pillow and the blue sky as his coverlet.

Cadwaladr and His Goat

CADWALADR had a very handsome goat named Jenny, of which he was very proud. Now Jenny was a very well-behaved goat as a rule and gave no trouble, but one evening she would not let Cadwaladr catch her. She ran round and round the field, and though Cadwaladr was fleet of foot, do what he would he could not get near her. Then she jumped over the hedge, like a hunter, into the next field. When Cadwaladr went after her, she jumped into the field beyond, and over the mountain wall towards the mountain. Several times she allowed Cadwaladr to come close up to her and then darted away. The last time she rushed up to the top of a high precipice. Cadwaladr, who had been getting wilder and wilder as his breath became shorter, now picked up a great stone and threw it at the exasperating animal with all his force. The stone knocked her over the precipice and she fell bleating to her doom. Cadwaladr was now very sorry, and made his way to the foot of the crag: the goat was dying, and licked his hand. This so affected him that he burst into tears, and sitting on the ground took the goat's head on his arm. Suddenly the goat was transformed into a beautiful young woman. Looking joyfully at him with great brown eyes, she said, "Ah, Cadwaladr, have I at last found you? Come with me." He put his hand in hers and allowed her to conduct him away. As for the hand, it felt just like a hoof, but when Cadwaladr looked at it, it seemed like an ordinary hand though it was whiter and more shapely than any hand he had ever seen before.

The maiden led him on and on, and Cadwaladr had never listened to more agreeable conversation than hers. At last they came to the top of a very high mountain. It was now night and the moon was shining. Cadwaladr looked round and saw that they were surrounded by a countless flock of goats, and the din of a most unearthly bleating arose suddenly. One of the goats which was larger than all the rest bleated as loudly as all the rest put together. This one rushed at Cadwaladr and, butting him in the stomach, sent him toppling over, just as he had sent Jenny. Cadwaladr went rolling down the mountain side and did not stop until his head went crash against a great rock. He fainted away and he did not recover consciousness until the sun and the singing birds awakened him in the morning. But he saw no more of either his goat or the fairy she had turned into from that day to his death.

The Fairy Wife

VERY many years ago there lived in the farmhouse of Ystrad, in Nant y Bettws, the Vale of the Beadhouse, a youth who was joyous and active, brave and determined of heart. On moonlight nights he used to amuse himself with watching the Fair Family dancing, and with listening to their music. One night they came very near the house, to a field near the lake, which was afterwards called Llyn y Dywarchen, the Lake of the Sod, there to beguile the night in merrymaking. The young fellow, as was his wont, went out to watch them. Immediately his eye fell on one of the fairy damsels, whose beauty was beyond anything he had ever seen in a human being. Her complexion was like blood upon snow: her voice was like the voice of a nightingale and as gentle as the breeze of a summer evening in a flower garden: her bearing was graceful and noble, and she tripped on the greensward as lightly as the rays of the sun had danced a few hours before on the ripples of the lake hard by. He fell in love with her over head and ears, and under the impulse of that sudden passion, when the merriment was at its height, he rushed into the middle of the fair crowd, snatched the lovely maiden in his arms, and ran off instantly with her into the house. As soon as the other fairies saw the violence that had been done by a mortal, they broke up the dance and ran off after her towards the house. But they were too late: the door was locked and bolted, and the stolen maiden was safely lodged in a chamber. The iron bolt and lock made it impossible for them to reclaim her, for the Fair Family abhor iron. When the young man had got her under his roof, he applied every means in his power to win her affection and asked her to marry him. She refused him, though he begged her time after time to be his wife. When, however, she saw that he would not allow her to return to her own people, she said to him, "I will not be your wife, but if you can find out my name I will be your servant." He, thinking that the task was by no means impossible, reluctantly agreed to the condition.

But the task was harder than he had imagined. He tried every name that he had ever heard of, even such curious Bible names as Zeruiah, La-ruhamel and Hazelel-poni, but found himself no nearer his point. Nevertheless, he was not willing to give up, and at last fortune came to his rescue. One night, as he was returning from Carnarvon market, he espied a number of the Fair Family in a turbary not far from his path. They seemed as if they were seriously deliberating together in council, and he at once thought to himself, "I am sure they are planning how to recover their stolen sister. Perhaps if I can get within hearing distance of them without being observed I shall be able to find out my darling's name."

On looking carefully around, he saw that a deep ditch ran through the turbary, and passed near the spot where the Fair Family sat in council. So he made his way round to the ditch and crept, on all fours, along it as quietly as a snail and almost as slowly, until he was within hearing of the group. After listening a while he found that he had been correct in his surmise: they were discussing the fate of the maiden whom he had carried away from them, and he heard one of them wailing aloud, "Oh, Penelope, Penelope, my sister, why didst thou run away with a mortal?"

"Penelope," said the young man to himself; "that must be the name of my beloved: that is enough." At once he began to creep back as quietly as he had crept there, and he managed to reach home without being seen by the fairies. When he got into the house he called out to the damsel, "Penelope, my heart of gold, come hither."

She came forward and asked in astonishment, "Oh, mortal, who has betrayed my name to thee?" Then folding her tiny hands, she exclaimed, "Alas, my fate, my fate!" But she resigned herself to her lot and took to her work as servant in earnest. Everything in the house and on the farm prospered under her charge. There was no better or cleaner housewife in all the country around, or one that was more provident and thrifty than she was. She milked the cows three times a day, and they gave the usual quantity of milk each time. The butter she made was so good that it fetched a penny a pound more than any other butter sold at Carnarvon market. The young man, however, was by no means willing that she should be a servant to him, and he persistently begged her to marry him. Many a blow will break the stone, says the Welsh proverb, and she at last consented to be married. But, said she, "There is one condition you must observe: you must never strike me with iron: if you do, I must be free to leave you and return to my family."

The young man would have agreed to any conditions, and this one he considered very easy to observe. So they were wedded, and lived happily together for years, and were blessed with two children, a boy and a girl, the images of their mother and the idols of their father. So wise and active was the fairy wife that he became one of the richest men of that country, and besides the farm of Ystrad he farmed all the lands on the north of Nant y Bettws to the top of Snowdon and all Cwm Brwynog, in Llanberis, or about five thousand acres.

One day the husband wanted to go to a fair at Carnarvon, and went out to catch a filly that was grazing in a field near the house, in order to sell her at the fair. But for the life of him he could not secure her, and he called to his wife to come to assist him. She came without delay, and they managed to drive the frisky young creature to a secure corner, as they thought: but, as he approached her to put on the bridle, the frolicsome animal rushed past him. In his anger he threw the bridle after her; but who should be running after her but his wife! The iron bit struck her on the cheek, and she vanished out of sight in a moment. But, though the broken compact had compelled her disappearance, the fairy wife could not forget her love for her children and husband. One cold night, a long time after this event, when the Dead Men's Feet Wind was blowing, the husband was awakened from his sleep by a gentle tapping on the glass of his bedroom window. After he had given a response he recognised the gentle and tender voice of his wife saying to him:

"Should the cold oppress my son,
See his father's coat's put on:
If my daughter feels the cold,
Wrap her in my skirt's thick fold."

She even contrived a way to see and speak to her loved ones regularly. The law of her country would not allow her to walk the earth after her return to Fairyland, so she made a large sod to float on the surface of the lake: on this she would spend hours and hours, freely conversing in tenderness with her husband and children on the shore. By means of this contrivance they managed to live together, until husband and children breathed their last. The floating island she made may still be seen, and it is from this that the lake acquired its name.

Einion and the Lady of the Greenwood

EINION, the son of Gwalchmai, was one fine summer day walking in the woods of Trefeilir, when he beheld a slender, graceful lady. Her complexion surpassed every white and red in the morning dawn, and the mountain snow, and every beautiful colour in the blossoms of wood, field and hill. Feeling in his heart a vast love he saluted her, and she returned the salutation, by which he perceived that his society was not disagreeable to her. He approached her in a courteous manner, and she also approached him. When he came near to her he saw that she had hoofs instead of feet, and would fain have fled. But she cast her glamour upon him and said, "Thou must follow me whithersoever I go." She had him in thrall, and he said he would go with her to the ends of the earth, but he requested of her permission first to go and bid farewell to his wife Angharad. This the Lady of the Greenwood agreed to, "but," said she, "I shall be with thee, invisible to all but to thyself."

So he went, and the goblin (for the Lady of the Greenwood was none other) went with him. When he saw Angharad his wife, she appeared an old hag, but he retained the recollection of days past and still felt true love for her, but he was not able to loose himself from the bond of his enchantment. "It is necessary for me," said he, "to part from thee for a time, I know not how long." They wept together and broke a gold ring between them: he kept one half and Angharad the other. They took their leave of each other, and he went with the Lady of the Greenwood and knew not whither: for a powerful spell was upon him, and he saw not any place or person or object under its true and proper appearance, excepting the half of the ring alone.

After being a long time, he knew not how long, with the Lady of the Greenwood, he looked one morning, as the sun was rising, upon the half of the ring, and he bethought him to place it in the most secret place he could find. He resolved to put it under his eyelid: as he was endeavouring to do so, he saw a man in white apparel and mounted on a snow-white horse coming towards him. The horseman asked him what he did there: Einion answered that he was cherishing the memory of his wife Angharad. "Dost thou desire to see her?" asked the man in white. "I do," replied Einion, "above all things and all pleasures in the world." "If so," said the man in white, "get upon this horse behind me." That Einion did, and looking around he could not see any trace of the Lady of the Greenwood, except the track of the hoofs of monstrous size, as if journeying towards the north. "What spell art thou under?" asked the man in white. Then Einion answered him and told everything, how it occurred betwixt him and the Lady of the Greenwood. "Take this white staff in thy hand, and wish for whatsoever thou desirest," said the man in white. Einion took it, and the first thing he wished was to see the Lady of the Greenwood, for he was not yet completely delivered from her spell. A hideous and uncanny beldam appeared to him, a thousand times more repulsive of aspect than the most frightful thing on earth. Einion uttered a cry of terror: the man in white cast his cloak over him, and in less than a twinkling Einion alighted on the hill of Trefeilir, by his own house, where he knew scarcely anyone, nor did anyone know him.

In the meantime, the goblin who had appeared to Einion as the Lady of the Greenwood had gone to Trefeilir in the form of an honourable and powerful nobleman, richly apparelled and wealthy. He placed a letter in Angharad's hand, in which it was stated that Einion had died in Norway more than nine years before. He cast his spell upon her, and she listened to his words of love. Soon, seeing that she should become a noble lady, higher than any in Wales, she named a day for her marriage with him. There was a great preparation of every elegant and sumptuous kind of apparel, and of meats and drinks, and of every excellence of song and instruments of music and festive entertainment.

Now, there was in Angharad's hall a very beautiful harp: when the goblin nobleman saw it, he wished to have it played, and the harpers who had assembled, the best in Wales, tried to put it in tune, but were not able. Just at this time Einion came into the house, and Angharad saw him as an old, decrepit, withered, grey-haired man, stooping with age, and dressed in rags. After the minstrels had failed to put the harp in tune, Einion took it in his hand and tuned it, and played on it an air which Angharad loved. She marvelled exceedingly, and asked him who he was. "I am Einion, the son of Gwalchmai," said he; "see, the bright gold is my token." And he gave her the ring. But she could not bring him to her recollection. Upon that he placed the white staff in Angharad's hand. Instantly the goblin, whom she had hitherto seen as a handsome and honourable nobleman, appeared to her as a monster, inconceivably hideous: she fainted from fear, and Einion supported her until she revived. When she opened her eyes, she saw neither the goblin nor any of the guests or minstrels, nothing except Einion and the harp and the banquet on the table, casting its savoury odour around. They sat down to eat, and exceeding great was their joy at the breaking of the spell which the goblin had cast over them.

There is a moral to this story, but it does not signify.

The Green Isles of the Ocean

THE people of Pembrokeshire were for a long time puzzled to know where the fairies, or the Children of Rhys the Deep, as they are called in Little England beyond Wales, lived. They used to attend the markets at Milford Haven and other places regularly. They made their purchases without speaking, laid down their money and departed, always leaving the exact sum required, which they seemed to know without asking the price of anything. A certain Gruffydd ab Einion was wont to supply them with more corn than anybody else, and there was one special butcher at Milford Haven upon whom they bestowed their patronage exclusively. To ordinary eyes they were invisible, but some keen-sighted persons caught glimpses of them at the markets; no one, however, saw them coming or going, and great was the curiosity as to where they lived, for even fairies must make their home somewhere.

One day Gruffydd ab Einion was walking about St. David's churchyard, when he saw islands far out at sea where he had never observed land before. "Ah!" he said, "there are the Green Isles of Ocean, Gwerddonau Llion, about which the poets sing. I will go to see them." He started to go down to the seashore to get a nearer view, but the islands disappeared. He went back to the place where he had seen the vision; he could again see the islands quite distinctly, with houses dotted here and there among green fields. Now, Gruffydd was a very acute man; he cut the turf from which he espied the islands, and took it down to a boat. He stood upon it, and, setting sail, before long landed on the shore of one of the islands. The fairies welcomed him warmly and, after showing him all the wonders of their home, sent him back loaded with presents. They made him, however, leave behind the enchanted turf, and pointed out an underground passage by which he could come to visit them. He continued to be a great friend of Rhys the Deep's children as long as he lived, and the gold they presented him with made him the richest man in West Wales.

March's Ears

MARCH ab Meirchion was lord of Castellmarch, in Lleyn. He ruled over leagues of rich land, tilled by hundreds of willing and obedient vassals. He had great possessions, fleet horses, greyhounds, hawks, countless black cattle and sheep, and a great herd of swine. (But few possessed pigs at that time, and their flesh was esteemed better than the flesh of oxen. Arthur himself sought to have one of March's sows.) In his palace he had much treasure of gold, silver, and Conway pearls, and all men envied him. But March was not happy: he had a secret, and day and night he was torn with dread lest it should be discovered. *He had horse's ears!*

To no one was the secret known except his barber. This man he compelled to take a solemn oath that he would not reveal his deformity to any living soul. If he wittingly or unwittingly should let anyone know that March's ears were other than human, March swore that he would cut his head off.

The barber became as unhappy as March: indeed his wretchedness was greater, because his fate would be worse if the secret were revealed. March would undergo ridicule, which is certainly a serious thing: but the barber would undergo decapitation, which is much more serious. The secret disagreed with his constitution so violently that he lost his appetite and his colour, and began to fall into a decline. So ill did he become that he had to call in a physician. This man was skilled in his craft, and he said to the barber, "You are being killed by a suppressed secret: unless you communicate it to someone you will soon be in your grave."

This announcement did not give the barber much consolation. He explained to the physician that if he did as he was directed he would lose his head. If in any event he had to come to the end of his earthly career, he preferred being interred with his head joined to, rather than separated from, his trunk. The physician then suggested that he should tell his secret to the ground. The barber thought there was not much danger to his cervical vertebræ (this is the learned name for neck bones) if he did this, and adopted the suggestion. He was at once relieved. His colour and appetite gradually came back, and before long he was as strong and well as he had ever been.

Now it happened that a fine crop of reeds grew on the spot where the barber whispered his secret to the ground. March prepared a great feast, and sent for one of Maelgwn Gwynedd's pipers, who was the best piper in the world, to make music for his guests. On his way to Castellmarch, the piper observed these fine reeds, and as his old pipe was getting worn out, he cut them and made an excellent new pipe. When his guests had eaten and drunk, March ordered the piper to play. What was the surprise of all when the pipe gave out no music, but only the words, "Horse's ears for March ab Meirchion, horse's ears for March ab Meirchion," over and over again. March drew his sword and would have slain the piper, but the hapless musician begged for mercy. He was not to blame, he said: he had tried to play his wonted music, but the pipe was charmed, and do what he would, he could get nothing out of it but the words, "Horse's ears for March ab Meirchion." March tried the pipe himself, but even he could not elicit any strains from it, but only the words, "Horse's ears for March ab Meirchion." So he forgave the piper and made no further effort to conceal his deformity.

The Fairy Harp

A COMPANY of fairies who lived in the recesses of Cader Idris were in the habit of going about from cottage to cottage in that part of the country to test the dispositions of the cottagers. Those who gave the fairies an ungracious welcome were subject to bad luck during the rest of their lives; but those who were good to the little folk who visited them in disguise received substantial favours from them.

Old Morgan ap Rhys was sitting one night by himself in his own chimney corner, solacing his loneliness with his pipe and some Llangollen ale. The generous liquor made Morgan very light-hearted, and he began to sing—at least he was under the impression that he was singing. His voice, however, was anything but sweet, and a bard whom he had offended—it is a very dangerous thing to fall foul of the bards in Wales, because they often have such bitter tongues—had likened his singing to the lowing of an old cow or the yelping of a blind dog which has lost its way to the cowyard. His singing, however, gave Morgan himself much satisfaction, and this particular evening he was especially pleased with the harmony he was producing. The only thing which marred his sense of contentment was the absence of an audience. Just as he was coming to the climax of his song, he heard a knock at the door. Delighted with the thought that there was someone to listen to him, Morgan sang with all the fervour he was capable of, and his top note was, in his opinion, a thing of beauty and a joy for ever. When he had quite finished, he again heard a knock at the door, and shouted out, "What is the door for but to come in by? Come in, whoever you are." Morgan's manners, you will see, were not very polished.

The door opened and in came three travellers, travel-stained and weary-looking. Now these were fairies from Cader Idris disguised in this manner to see how Morgan treated strangers, but he never suspected they were other than they appeared. "Good sir," said one of the travellers, "we are worn and tired, but all we seek is a bite of food to put in our wallets, and then we will go on our way."

"Brensiach," said Morgan, "is that all you want? Well, there, look you, is the loaf and the cheese, and the knife lies by them, and you cut what you like. Eat your heartiest and fill your wallets, for never shall it be said that Morgan ap Rhys denied bread and cheese to strangers that came into his house." The travellers proceeded to help themselves, and Morgan, determined not to fail in hospitality, sang to them while they ate, moistening his throat occasionally with Llangollen ale when it became dry.

The fairy travellers, after they had regaled themselves sufficiently, got up to go and said, "Good sir, we thank you for our entertainment. Since you have been so generous we will show that we are grateful. It is in our power to grant you any one wish you may have: tell us what that wish may be."

"Well, indeed," said Morgan, "the wish of my heart is to have a harp that will play under my fingers, no matter how ill I strike it: a harp that will play lively tunes, look you—no melancholy music for me. But surely it's making fun of me you are."

But that was not the case: he had hardly finished speaking when, to his astonishment, there on the hearth before him stood a splendid harp. He looked round and found his guests had vanished. "That's the most extraordinary thing I have ever seen in my life," said Morgan, "they must have been fairies," and he was so flabbergasted that he felt constrained to drink some more ale. This allayed to some extent his bewilderment, and he proceeded to try the instrument he had been so mysteriously presented with. As soon as his fingers touched the strings, the harp began to play a mad and capering tune. Just then there was a sound of footsteps, and in came his wife with some friends. No sooner did they hear the strains of the harp than they began dancing, and as long as Morgan's fingers were on the strings, they kept footing it like mad creatures.

The news that Morgan had come into possession of a harp with some mysterious power spread like wildfire over the whole country, and many were the visitors who came to see him and it. Every time he played it everyone felt irresistibly impelled to dance, and could not leave off until Morgan stopped. Even lame people capered away, and a one-legged man who visited him danced as merrily as any biped.

One day, among the company who had come to see if the stories about the harp were true, was the bard who had made such unpleasant remarks about Morgan's singing. Morgan determined to pay him out, and instead of stopping as usual after the dance had been going on for a few minutes, he kept on playing. He played on and on until the dancers were exhausted and shouted to him to stop. But Morgan was finding the scene such too amusing to want to stop. He laughed until his sides ached and the tears rolled down his cheeks at the antics of his visitors, and especially at those of the bard. The longer he played the madder became the dance: the dancers spun round and round, wildly knocking over the furniture, and some of them bounded up against the roof of the cottage till their heads cracked again. Morgan did not stop until the bard had broken his legs and the rest had been jolted almost to pieces. By that time his revenge was satisfied, and his sides and jaws were so tired with laughing that he had to take his fingers away from the strings.

But this was the last time he was to have the chance of venting his spite on his enemies. By next morning the harp had disappeared, and was never seen again. The fairies, evidently displeased with the evil use to which their gift had been put, must have taken it away in the night. And this is a warning to all who abuse the gifts of the fairies.

Guto Bach and the Fairies

GRUFFYDD was the name given at baptism to a little boy who once lived at Llangybi, but everyone called him Guto Bach. One day, after he had been up to the mountain to see his father's sheep, he brought home a number of pieces, the size of crowns, with letters stamped on them and resembling real crown pieces exactly, only that they were made of white paper instead of silver. His mother asked him where he had got them. "I played with some little children on the mountain," said little Guto, "and they gave them to me." "Whose children?" asked the mother. "I don't know," he replied; "they are very nice children, much nicer than I am." But his mother knew they were fairies, and told him he must never go on the mountain again by himself, because no good ever came of playing with strange children.

But Guto was longing to have another game with the little children. One day he disobeyed his mother and slipped away to the mountain. He did not come back, and though every search was made for him, no trace of Guto Bach could be found anywhere. Two years after, however, what should his mother see on opening the door in the morning but little Guto sitting on the threshold with a bundle under his arm. He was the very same size and dressed in the same little clothes as on the day of his disappearance, and he did not look a day older. "My child," said the astonished and delighted mother, "where have you been this long, long while?" "Mother," said Guto, "I have not been long away; it was only yesterday that I went to play with the little children. Look what pretty clothes they have given me." The mother opened the bundle; it contained a dress of very white paper without seam or sewing. As it had been given to him by the fairies she burnt it, and Guto's long disappearance made her more sure that no good could come of playing with strange children.

But she was wrong all the same. Guto Bach's friendship with the little children, as he still thought they were, proved to be very advantageous. Shortly after his reappearance his father and mother suffered a very great loss. They had invested all their savings and all the money they could raise in a ship sailing from Pwllheli, which had been making very profitable voyages and bringing great wealth to those who had shares in her. The vessel went down in a storm, and ruin stared Guto's parents in the face. Now there was on Pentyrch, the hill above Llangybi, a great rock under which there was said to be a great treasure of gold hidden. Many men had tried to move the rock, but had failed because they were undeserving. Guto's father determined to make another effort to dislodge the stone, in the hope that the treasure underneath it would recoup his losses. His neighbours sympathised with him, and brought all the horses of the parish to help him. But the rock was so heavy and fixed so fast in the ground that the combined efforts of all the men and horses of Llangybi were unavailing. Guto's father's hopes had been high: whatever the others might have been who had attempted to reach the treasure, he at least, he thought, was deserving. The disappointment, therefore, was all the harder to bear.

Seeing his parents' grief, Guto remembered that the little children with whom he had played had plenty of gold and silver, and he made up his mind to ask them to help his father and mother in their distress. He went again to the mountain and found the little children playing as before. He told them his trouble, and asked them whether they could spare him some of their money. "No," they said, "there is plenty of gold and silver waiting for you under the rock on Pentyrch." "But," remonstrated little Guto, "it would not budge for all the men and horses of Llangybi." "We are aware of that," said the little children, "but do you try to move it and see what will happen."

Guto went home and told his parents what the little children had said to him. They laughed at the idea that little Guto would succeed where the full strength of Llangybi parish had failed. But they were in such a desperate plight that they allowed Guto to do as the fairies had directed. They took him to the rock. He put his little hand on it, and the great mass trembled. He gave it a shove, and the huge stone crashed down the hill. Underneath it there was found enough gold and silver not only to replace all their losses, but to make Guto and his parents the richest people in Carnarvonshire.

Ianto's Chase

MANY, many years ago, there was a man in the hills of Breconshire whose proper name was Ifan Sion Watkin, but he was more generally known as Ianto Coedcae, Ianto being a nickname for Ifan, and Coedcae being the name of the farm at which he lived.

Ianto was invited to the house of a friend on the borders of Glamorgan to celebrate a christening. He accepted the invitation gladly, expecting to have a jolly evening. Nor was he disappointed. There were plenty of good things to eat: there was abundance of strong ale and old mead to drink: there was dancing and penillion were sung to the harp. The time passed so quickly that it was quite a shock to Ifan to hear the old clock in the corner striking twelve. He had urgent business to attend to at home next morning, and as he had a long way to go he began to make preparations for going.

His host looked out into the night. "Ianto," he said, "it is as dark as a cow's inside. Will you have a lantern to light you home?"

Ianto felt insulted. "Do you take me for a child?" he asked indignantly. "I have been out on nights so dark that I could not see my hand in front of me, and I have never failed to find my way home. A lantern for me? No, thank you."

After bidding good-night to the other guests, who having only a short distance to go were in no hurry to put an end to the festivities, and to his host and hostess, Ianto set off at a rattling pace for his home over the mountain. He had walked some time and covered the best portion of his journey when he thought he could hear at a great distance some sounds resembling music nearly in the direction he was going. As he advanced Ianto found himself approaching these sounds so near that he could plainly distinguish them as proceeding from a harp and some voices singing to it. He could even make out the tune, which was, Ar hyd y Nos—All through the Night. Ianto laughed. "Jabox," he said, "that is a very appropriate tune." The remark he had made struck him as most apposite, and he laughed again right merrily.

He tried to discover who they were who were thus amusing themselves, but could not do so on account of the darkness. As he knew there was no house within a great distance of that spot his curiosity was greatly excited. The music still continuing and seemingly but a short distance from the path, he thought there could be no harm in deviating a little out of his way in order to see what was going forward. Moreover, he thought that it would be a pity to pass so near such a merry party without giving them the opportunity of inviting him to join in their mirth. Accordingly he made an oblique cut in the direction of the music, and having gone fully as far as the place from which he was quite sure the sounds emanated when he left the path, he was not a little surprised to find that they were still at some distance from him.

"This is curious," said Ianto, and he was so puzzled that he scratched his head vigorously for a minute or two. This cleared his intellect, and he wondered why he had been so slow to realise the explanation of the difficulty. "There's dull I am," he said, "not to remember that sounds are heard at a much greater distance by night than by day. That is how it is, of course."

Off he started again, but somehow or other the more he walked the less chance he saw of getting there. He stopped to think things over. The music at this time was quite a long way off and receding from him. "No," he said, "I will not give it up," and he quickened his pace lest he should lose the strains altogether. He had not gone more than ten yards when a strange thing happened. He tumbled up to his neck in a turf bog. When he had struggled out and tidied himself up as well as he could under the circumstances, the music struck up quite near him, and he heard his name called, "Ifan, Ifan."

This was the most respectful mode of addressing him, and he reflected, "Well, whoever they are, they must be well-bred people." Instead of giving up the chase, as he had fully intended to do after his accident, he became more desirous than ever of joining a company which was evidently as polite as it was harmonious. On he walked, and in a minute or two he heard himself called, "Ianto, Ianto." This was not such a dignified appellation as "Ifan, Ifan," but he was in such a clever mood that he had no difficulty in arriving at the explanation. "There must be someone in the company who knows me intimately," he said, and he therefore concluded that the familiarity was excusable. The salutations, however, which seemed to alternate between "Ifan, Ifan," and "Ianto, Ianto," now became so indistinct that he could not always decide whether or not they proceeded from the grouse or the lapwings which he was continually disturbing among the heather.

At length, chagrined and mortified by his repeated disappointments and excessively fatigued, he determined to lie down on the ground till morning. But he had scarcely composed himself to sleep when the harp struck up again more brilliantly than ever, and seemed so near that he could plainly hear the words of the song that was being sung to it. Upon this he started up, absolutely determined, come what may, to achieve his quest. He tumbled into bogs, waded knee-deep through water, and scratched his legs in labouring through heather and gorse, but his blood was up and he did not mind. Suddenly he saw at a small distance from him a number of lights, which on a nearer approach he found to proceed from a house in which there appeared to be a large company assembled, enjoying a similar merrymaking to the one he had left, with music, with drink, and other good cheer. At the door a very bonny lass invited him in, seated him in a comfortable armchair by a roaring fire, and asked him whether he would have ale or mead. Ianto thought that ale would pick him up after his long walk rather better than mead, and the maid bustled away to fetch it. But before it arrived, or he had time to take stock of the company around him, such was the effect of the fatigue he had undergone that he fell fast asleep.

He was awakened next morning by the sunbeams playing on his face. On opening his eyes and looking around him, he was more than astonished to find himself quite alone. The house and the convivial company had completely vanished, and not a vestige remained of what he had positively seen before going to sleep. Instead of being comfortably seated in a good armchair by a roaring fire, he found himself almost frozen with cold and lying on a bare rock on the point of one of the loftiest crags of Mynydd Pen Cyrn, a thousand feet in height, down which poor Ianto would have fallen headlong had he moved but a foot or two further.

The Stray Cow

In a secluded spot in the upland country behind Aberdovey is a small lake called Llyn Barfog, or the Lake of the Bearded One. Its waters are black and gloomy, no fish is ever seen to rise to the surface, and the fowls of the air fly high above it.

In times of old the neighbourhood of the lake was haunted by a band of elfin ladies. They were sometimes seen in the dusk of a summer evening, clad all in green, accompanied by their hounds and comely milk-white kine; but no one was favoured with more than a passing glimpse till an old farmer residing at Dyssyrnant, in the adjoining valley of Dyffryn Gwyn, had the good luck to catch one of the Gwartheg y Llyn, or kine of the lake, which had fallen in love with the cattle of his herd. From the day that he captured the elfin cow the farmer's fortune was made. Never was there such a cow, never such calves, never such milk and butter and cheese, and the fame of the Fuwch Gyfeiliorn, or the Stray Cow, spread through that central part of Wales known as Rhwng y Ddwy Afon, the Mesopotamia between the banks of the Mawddach and those of the Dovey. The farmer, who had been poor, became rich, the owner of vast flocks and herds, a very patriarch of the mountains.

But much wealth made him mad. Fearing that the elfin cow would become too old to be profitable, he thought that he had better fatten her for the market. Even when she was fattened she showed that she was different from earthly cattle, for never was such a fat beast seen as this cow grew to be. Killing day came, and the neighbours came from all about to see it slaughtered.

The cow was tethered, no regard being paid to her mournful lowing and pleading eyes. The farmer counted up his gains from the sale, and the butcher raised his red right arm to strike the fatal blow. Just as the bludgeon was falling, a piercing cry awakened the echoes of the hills and made the welkin ring. The butcher's arm was paralysed and the bludgeon fell from his hand. Looking in the direction from which the shriek had come, the astonished assemblage beheld a female figure, clad in green, with uplifted arms, standing on one of the crags overhanging Llyn Barfog, and heard her calling with a voice loud as thunder:

> "Come thou, Einion's Yellow One,
> Stray-horns, the Particoloured Lake Cow,
> And the hornless Dodyn,
> Arise, come home."

No sooner were these words uttered than the elfin cow and all her progeny to the third and fourth generation were in full flight towards the lake. Partly recovering from his astonishment, the farmer ran his hardest after them, but when, breathless and panting, he gained an eminence overlooking the water, he saw the elfin dame, with the cows and their calves formed in a circle round her, leisurely descending mid-lake. They disappeared beneath the dark surface, leaving only the yellow water-lily to mark the spot where they had vanished.

The farmer was reduced from wealth to poverty, but few felt pity for one who had shown himself so ungrateful as to purpose slaying his benefactor.

Bala Lake

LONG, long ago, there was a fertile valley where now roll the waters of Bala Lake.

In a stately palace in the middle of the valley lived a cruel and unjust prince. "As a roaring lion and a ranging bear, so is a wicked ruler over the poor people." He feared not God, neither regarded man, and he so oppressed and vexed the five parishes of Penllyn that his name stank in the nostrils of the men of Meirion.

Those whom he afflicted cried to the Lord, and He sent a warning to the oppressor. As the wicked ruler walked in his garden he heard a voice saying, "Vengeance will come," but he laughed the warning to scorn. And he seemed to have reason, for he flourished exceedingly. He laid up treasure and took to wife a noble lady, who bore him a son.

To celebrate the birth of his first-born he prepared a splendid feast, and sent his servants to bid the highest in the land to it. Many made excuse, but many came, and they supped sumptuously. Every sort of meat and every sort of liquor was served that was ever seen elsewhere, and no vessel was placed upon the table that was not either of gold, or of silver, or of buffalo horn. Merry tales were told and mirthful songs were sung, and when it was more agreeable to them to dance than to listen to tales and songs, they danced to the strains of the harp.

About midnight there was an interval in the dancing and the harper was resting alone in a corner, when suddenly he heard a whisper in his ear, "Vengeance, vengeance."

He turned at once, and saw a little bird hovering about him. Having arrested the harper's attention, the bird flew slowly to the door. The harper did not go after it, and the bird came back, sang plaintively a second time in his ear, "Vengeance, vengeance," after which it again flew off to the door, beckoning, as it were, to the harper to follow. This time the harper went after it, but after getting outside he hesitated. Once more the bird returned to him and piped, "Vengeance, vengeance," mournfully and sadly in his ear.

The harper now became afraid of refusing to follow, and proceeded to walk in the direction in which the bird invited him to advance. On they went, through thicket and through bog, the bird hovering the while in front of him and leading him along the easiest and safest paths. If he but stopped for a moment the bird would sing, "Vengeance, vengeance," and he felt constrained to continue his flight. At last he reached the top of a hill, some considerable distance from the palace. By this time he was fatigued and weary (for he was an old man), and he stopped to rest. He fully expected to hear the bird's warning note as before, but on this occasion, though he listened carefully, he could hear nothing but the murmuring of the little burn hard by.

"How foolish I have been," he now thought to himself, "to allow myself to be led away in this fashion from the palace! They will be looking for me to play for the next dance and I must hurry back."

In his anxiety, however, to make haste, the old harper lost his way on the hill, and found himself forced to await the break of day.

When the sun's rim appeared above the Berwyn mountains, he turned his eye in the direction of the palace. He was astonished beyond measure to see no trace of it. The whole valley was one calm, large lake, and he could descry his harp floating on the face of the waters.

The Forbidden Fountain

THERE was once a boy of twelve years of age who was often sent by his father to tend the sheep on the Frenni fach. Early one morning in June he drove the sheep to their pasture for the day and looked carefully at the top of the Frenni fawr to see which way the morning fog was declining. Young as he was, he was weather-wise, and knew that if the fog declined to the Pembrokeshire side it would be a fine day, whereas if it went to the Cardiganshire side the weather would be foul. The fog was going to the Pembrokeshire side, and the boy, delighted with the prospect of a fine day, was whistling a merry tune and looking idly about him, when he saw at a considerable distance away what seemed to be a party of soldiers busily engaged in some operation, the nature of which he could not make out at first.

"There cannot be any soldiers on the mountain as early as this," he reflected, and going to the top of a little hillock, he perceived that they were too small for soldiers. "I wonder whether they are the Fair Family," he said. He had often heard of them and had seen their rings, but he had never set eyes on the little people themselves. First of all, he thought of running home to tell his father and mother, but reflecting that they might disappear before he returned and that perhaps his parents might even forbid him to come back—for many people were afraid of the Fair Family—he dismissed that idea. After cogitating for a little while he determined to go as near them as he could, and by degrees he arrived within a short distance of the visitors, where he remained for some time observing their motions. The visitors were tiny little people of both sexes, and they were the most handsome people he had ever seen. Some of them were dancing, whirling round and round in a ring with joined hands. Others were chasing one another with surprising swiftness, and others again were galloping about on small white horses. Their dresses varied in colour, some being white and others scarlet. The little men wore red tripled caps and the little women a light head-dress, which waved fantastically in the breeze. All were laughing gleefully, and as merry as could be.

Before long they noticed the boy, and, with laughing faces, beckoned him to join them. So he gradually went nearer, till at length he ventured to place one foot in the circle. No sooner had he done so than his ears were charmed with the most melodious music in the world, and he moved his other foot into the circle.

The instant he did this, he found himself, not in a fairy ring on the mountain side, but in a magnificent palace glittering with gold and pearls. Every form of beauty surrounded him, and every variety of pleasure was offered him. He was free to range wherever he pleased, and his every movement was waited on by maidens of matchless loveliness. Instead of the tatws a llaeth (potatoes and butter-milk) and the flummery to which he had hitherto been accustomed, here were the choicest viands, served on silver plates, and instead of small beer, the only kind of intoxicating liquor he had before tasted, here were red and yellow wines of wondrous enjoyableness, brought in golden goblets richly inlaid with gems. There was only one restriction on his freedom: he was not to drink on any consideration from a certain fountain in the garden, in which swam fishes of golden and other colours. Each day new joys were provided for him; new pastimes were invented to charm him and new faces presented themselves, more lovely, if possible, than those he had seen before.

Possessing everything that mortal could desire, the boy still wanted the one thing forbidden. Like Eve in the Garden of Eden, he was undone by curiosity. One day he was near the fountain, gazing at the fishes sporting in the water. There was nobody looking on, and he plunged his hand into the fountain:

the fishes all disappeared instantly. He put the water to his mouth: a confused shriek ran through the garden. He drank: the palace and all vanished, and he found himself on the mountain in the very place where he first entered the ring. The sheep were grazing just where he had left them, and the fog on the mountain had scarcely moved. He thought he had been absent for many years, but he had only been away so many minutes.

Tudur ap Einion

HALF-WAY up the ascent from Llangollen to Dinas Bran, or Bran's Fortress (the wicked man who called it Crow Castle ought to have been hanged, drawn and quartered), lies a hollow known by the name of Nant yr Ellyllon, the Elves' Dell. Once upon a time a young man, who was known as Tudur ap Einion Gloff, used to pasture his master's sheep in this hollow. One summer night Tudur was preparing to return to the lowlands with his woolly charge, when he suddenly saw, perched on a stone near him, a little man in moss breeches with a fiddle under his arm. He was the tiniest wee specimen of humanity imaginable. His coat was made of birch leaves, and he wore upon his head a helmet consisting of a gorse flower, while his feet were encased in shoes made of beetles' wings. He ran his fingers over his instrument, and the music made Tudur's hair stand on end. "Nos dawch, nos dawch," said the little man (this means in English, "Good night to you, good night to you.") "Ac i chwithau," replied Tudur, which is, being interpreted, "The same to you." Then continued the little man, "You are fond of dancing, Tudur: and if you but tarry awhile you shall behold some of the best dancers in Wales. I," added the little man, swelling his chest out, "I am a musician." "Where is your harp?" asked Tudur, "a Welshman cannot dance without a harp." "Harp?" repeated the wee being scornfully, "I can discourse better music for dancing upon my fiddle." "Is it a fiddle," rejoined Tudur, "that you call that stringed wooden spoon in your hand?" He had never seen such an instrument before. And now Tudur beheld through the dusk hundreds of pretty little sprites converging from all parts of the mountain towards the spot where they stood. Some were dressed in white and some in blue and some in pink, and some carried glow-worms in their hands as torches. So lightly did they tread that not a blade of grass nor any flower was crushed beneath their weight, and all made a curtsey or a bow to Tudur as they passed. Tudur was not to be outdone in politeness, and he doffed his cap and bowed to each in return.

Presently the little minstrel drew his bow across the strings of his instrument, and the music produced was so enchanting that Tudur stood transfixed to the spot. Then at the sound of the sweet melody the fairies, if fairies they were, ranged themselves in groups and began to dance, and as the minstrel quickened his bow the dancers went round and round. Now, of all the dancing Tudur had ever seen, none came near the dancing of the fairies. It was the very poetry of motion. Sian Lan was the best dancer within ten miles of Llangollen, and Tudur had often had a turn with her at the merry nights in Glyn Ceiriog, but Sian's dancing was clumsy and heavy compared with what he now saw. He felt an itching in his feet and could not help keeping time to the merry music, but he was afraid to join in the dance. He wanted to go to Heaven in good time, though he was in no particular hurry, and it occurred to him that it might not be the most direct route to Paradise to dance on a mountain at night in strange company, to, perhaps, the devil's fiddle. The music became faster and the dance wilder, and Tudur's whole body kept time.

"Dance away, Tudur," cried the little man. But Tudur was too wary. "Nay, nay," he said, "dance on, my little beauties, while I look on and admire." The music became sweeter and the dance more enticing than before. Tudur looked on, more absorbed than ever, and his feet and hands became more and more excited. At last, losing all control over himself, he went into the middle of the ring. "Now for it," he shouted, throwing his cap into the air. "Play away, fiddler."

No sooner were these words uttered than everything underwent a change. The gorse-blossom cap vanished from the minstrel's head, and a pair of goat's horns branched out instead. His face became as black as soot: a long tail grew out of his leafy coat and cloven hoofs replaced the beetle-wing pumps. Tudur's heart was heavy, but his heels were light. Horror was in his bosom, but irresistible motion was in his feet. The fairies changed into a variety of forms. Some became goats and some became dogs, some assumed the shape of foxes and others that of cats. It was the strangest crew that ever surrounded a human being. The dance became at last so furious that Tudur could not make out the forms of the dancers. They whirled round him with such rapidity that they resembled a wheel of fire. Tudur danced on and on. He could not stop, for the devil's music was too much for him, as the figure with the goat's horns poured it out of the strings of his fiddle with unceasing vigour. It went on thus throughout the night.

Next morning Tudur's master went up the mountain to see what had become of his sheep and his shepherd. He found the flock safe and sound, but was astonished to see Tudur spinning like mad in the middle of the hollow by himself. "Stop me, master, stop me," shouted Tudur to him. "Stop yourself," replied he. "What is the matter with you, in the name of Heaven?" At the word Tudur fell panting and exhausted at his master's feet, and it was long before he recovered his breath and his senses sufficiently to explain his strange conduct.

The Fairy Walking Stick

A FARMER was rounding up his sheep in Cwmllan when he heard the sound of weeping. As a general rule, only human beings weep noisily, and as the farmer had not observed any human beings in the vicinity he was considerably surprised. He went in the direction from which the sound came. For some time he could not discover who was causing it, but after a bit he saw a wee little lass lying on a narrow ledge of rock on the face of a great precipice, and sobbing as if her heart would break. He went to her rescue, and with great difficulty extricated her from her dangerous position. No sooner had he brought her to safety, than a little old man appeared. "I thank thee," said he, "for thy kindness to my daughter. Accept this in remembrance of thy good deed," handing a walking stick to the farmer. The farmer took it, and the moment it was in his hand both the wee lass and the little old man disappeared from his sight.

The year after this every sheep in the farmer's possession had two ewe-lambs, and this continued for many years. His flocks during all this time were singularly free from accident and disease. Sheep-stealers were always frustrated in their evil designs upon them: birds of prey never ventured near them to pick out the eyes of the young lambs: even when a murrain devastated other flocks, these were untainted: when they were buried under snowdrifts in winter, and had to be dug out, they seemed better rather than worse for their experiences: and their wool was finer and more plentiful than that of any other sheep in the country. The farmer became rich, and all envied him.

One night, shortly after the sheep had been brought down from the mountains for the winter, the farmer went to a village some distance away to match his blue game-cock against a black fighter which was carrying all before it. It was late before the farmer started home, and a great storm arose. The wind howled, and the rain came down in sheets, and a horror of great darkness fell upon the land. On his way home the farmer had to cross a stream on some stepping stones. When he came to it the river was swollen, and sweeping all before it in a swift current. As he was feeling for the stones with the walking stick given him by the little old man, it somehow or other slipped from his hand and was swept away by the raging torrent, and he had a narrow escape of being carried away himself.

He reached home, and as soon as day came went out to search for the stick, and at the same time to see what damage had been done by the flood. He found that nearly all his sheep had been swept away by it. His wealth had gone as it came—with the walking stick.

Dick the Fiddler's Money

DICK the Fiddler used to spend on drink all the money he earned by playing at merrymakings, weddings and fairs. After a week's fuddle at Darowen he was one night wending his way home to his wife and children. He had to go through Fairy Green Lane, just above the farmstead of Cefn Cloddiau, and when he came to it he felt nervous. To banish fear he tuned his beloved instrument, and as he walked along he played his favourite air, "The Crow's Black Wing." When he passed the greensward where the fairies used to revel he felt his fiddle suddenly becoming very heavy, and he heard a rattling and a tinkling inside it. This continued until he reached Llwybr Scriw Riw, his home. When he entered the cottage he had to listen to harsher music than he was wont to extract from his fiddle, to wit, the angry voice of his wife, who, justly angered at his absence, began to lecture and scold him. He was called names which he richly deserved: idler, fool, drunken sot, and so forth. "How is it possible," asked his wife, "for me to beg enough for myself and half a houseful of children nearly naked, while you go about the country spending on drink the little money you earn? The landlord came here this morning, and said that if you do not pay him the rent which has long been overdue he will turn us all out, and what are we to do then? I am sure you have spent all your earnings as usual on beer, and that you haven't got a ha'penny in your pocket." "Hush, hush, my good woman," said Dick, "see what's in my old fiddle." She obeyed, shook it, and out tumbled a number of bright new five-shilling pieces, more than enough to pay the rent. She promptly put the money away in a safe place, and asked him how he had come into possession of it, and he told her.

The following day he went to Llanidloes to pay his rent. His landlord was more than surprised to find that Dick had come, not to beg for mercy, as he had done several times before, but to discharge his debt. He gave him a receipt, and thirsty Dick betook himself to the "Unicorn" to sample Betty Brunt's ale before returning home. He had not consumed more than a trifle of half-a-dozen glasses when in came his landlord in a state of great excitement. "Where did you get the money you gave me?" he asked. "Why, what's the matter with it?" asked Dick. "It has turned into cockleshells," said the landlord. "Well, it was all right when I gave it to you, and here is the receipt," said Dick, flourishing the document triumphantly. "Somebody must have bewitched the coins." He vouchsafed no further explanation, and even when he was gloriously drunk, as he finished up the evening by becoming, no one was able to pump any information out of him as to the origin of the money he had given the landlord.

A Strange Otter

ONE day two friends went to hunt otters on the banks of the Pennant, in Merionethshire. When they were yet some distance from the river they saw some small creature of a red colour, running fast across the meadows in the direction of the stream. Off they ran after it, but before they could catch it the little animal hid itself beneath the roots of a tree, on the brink of a river. The two men thought it was an otter, but at the same time they could not understand why it was red. They thought they would like to catch such an extraordinary specimen alive, and one of them said to the other, "You go home to get a sack, while I watch." Now, there were two holes under the roots of the tree, and while one held the sack with its mouth open over one of them, the other pushed his stick into the other hole. Presently the creature went into the sack, and the two men set out for home, thinking they had achieved a great feat. Before they had proceeded the width of one field the inmate of the sack spoke in a sad voice, and said: "My mother is calling for me: oh, my mother is calling for me!" This gave the two hunters a great fright, and they at once threw down the sack. Great was their surprise when they saw a little man in a red dress running out of the sack towards the water. He disappeared from their sight in the bushes by the river. The two men were greatly terrified, and felt that it was more prudent to go home than meddle any further with the Fair Family.

Fairy Ointment

THE old couple who lived at the Garth Dorwen went to Carnarvon to hire a servant maid at the Allhallows' Fair. They went to the spot where the young men and women who wanted places were accustomed to station themselves, and saw a lass with golden hair, standing a little apart from all the others. They asked her if she wanted a place: she replied that she did, and she hired herself at once and came to her place at the time fixed. Her name, she said, was Eilian.

In those days it was customary to spin after supper during the long winter months. Now Eilian, on nights when the moon was shining, would take her wheel down to the meadow, and the Fair Family used to come to help her. On these occasions an enormous amount of spinning was done, and great was the joy of the old couple at having secured such a maid-servant.

But their fortune was too good to last: in the spring when the days grew long Eilian disappeared. Everyone thought that she had gone with the Fair Family, and for once everyone was right. Now this is how it was found out for certain that Eilian was with the fairies. The old woman of Garth Dorwen was by way of being a nurse, and some time after Eilian's disappearance, on a night when the moon was full and there was a little rain falling through a thin mist, a gentleman on horseback came to fetch her. So she rode off behind the stranger on his horse and came to Rhos y Cowrt. The two dismounted and entered a great cave, and through a door at the far end of it passed into a bed-chamber, where a lady lay in her bed: it was the finest place the old woman had ever seen in her life.

The old woman saw and heard nobody there but the gentleman who had fetched her, the mother and the baby. This was curious, because she found dainty food prepared for the mother, and everything she wanted was procured by some invisible power. The mystery was not solved until one morning the husband gave her a bottle of ointment to anoint the baby's eyes with. "Take care," he said, "that you do not touch your own eyes with it, or evil will befall you." The old woman promised to be careful, but somehow or other, after putting the bottle by, her left eye began to itch, and without thinking what she was doing she rubbed it with the same finger that she had used for the baby's eyes. And now a strange thing happened: with the right eye she saw everything as before, gorgeous and luxurious as the heart could wish, but with the left eye she saw a damp, miserable cave, and lying on some rushes and withered ferns, with big stones all round her, was her former servant-girl, Eilian. In the course of the day she saw a great deal more. There were small men and small women going in and out, their movements being as light as the morning breeze. They prepared dainties with the utmost skill and rapidity, and served Eilian with a kindness and affection that was truly remarkable.

In the evening the old woman said, "You have had a great many visitors to-day, Eilian."

"Yes," was the reply, "but how do you know me?" Then the old woman explained that she had accidentally rubbed her left eye with the baby's ointment.

"Take care that my husband does not find out that you recognise me," said Eilian, and she told the old woman her story. She had been helped with her spinning by the fairies on condition that she married one of them. "I never meant to carry out the agreement," she added, "And I used to draw a knife whenever they pestered me too much about it on the meadow. That made them vanish immediately. And for fear they should carry me off when I was asleep, I placed a long stick of mountain ash regularly across my bed, for no fairy dares touch or cross a branch of the rowan tree. That kept me safe so long that I grew careless, and the day we sheared the sheep I was so tired that I forgot to protect my bed. That very night I was whisked off to Fairyland."

The old woman was very cautious after Eilian's warning, and gave the fairy husband no inkling that her left eye had any different power of vision from the right. Her time came to an end without mishap, and she was taken home on horseback just as she had come, and she was given a fine sum of money for her services.

Some time after the old woman was late in getting to market. When she arrived a friend said to her, "The fairies must be here to-day; the noise is swelling and prices are rising." Sure enough the fairies were there, but they were invisible to all eyes except the old woman's left eye. She saw Eilian's husband stealing something from a stall close by her: she went up to him and, forgetting the warning, said, "Good morning, master, how is Eilian?" "She is quite well," replied the fairy, "but with what eye do you see me?" "With this," said the old woman, pointing to her left. The fairy immediately put out her eye with a bulrush, and her right eye had to do the work of two all the rest of her life.

Pergrin and the Mermaiden

ONE fine September afternoon, about the beginning of the eighteenth century, a fisherman of St. Dogmael's, whose name was Pergrin, was rowing in his boat near Pen Cemmes. Looking up at the rocks casually, he thought he saw a maiden in a recess of the cliff. Pergrin was an inquisitive man, and he determined to see what the strange lady was doing. He rowed ashore as quietly as he could, stepped out of his boat and crawled up to a place where he could see into the recess without being seen himself. He espied a lovely maiden—at least, above the waist she was a lovely maiden, but below the waist she was a fish with fins and spreading tail. She was combing her long hair so busily and intently that she had no suspicion that she was being watched, and Pergrin gazed upon her for a long time. During that time his mind was active, and he determined to carry her away. Putting his revolve into action, Pergrin rushed at her, and taking her up in his arms, carried her off to his boat. There he fastened her securely, and turning his boat's nose in the direction of Llandudoch (that is the Welsh for St. Dogmael's), began to ply his oars vigorously. When she realized her situation, being a woman (at least, as far as the waist) she wept, and begged Pergrin to let her go. Pergrin, however, though he answered her very kindly, would not accede to her tearful request, but carried her home and shut her up in a room. He treated her very tenderly, but she refused all meat and drink (she rejected even the best *cawl*, with hundreds of eyes in it), and did nothing but shed tears and beseech Pergrin to release her. A famous man once said that as much pity is to be taken of a woman weeping as of a goose going barefoot, but Pergrin had never heard this saying: it would have made no difference if he had, for he was soft-hearted, and the sight of the beauteous half-woman's eyes becoming red, and her nose swollen with the constant drip of salt water, affected him profoundly. Moreover, as she persistently declined food, she became thin and peakish. To add to his anxiety, a friend of his, who knew far too much to be a pleasant companion, told him what had happened to a man in Conway who caught a mermaid. She prayed him to place her tail at least in the water, but he refused, and she died. Before dying she cursed her captor and the place of her imprisonment. The captor had gone from bad to worse, and had perished miserably: the people of Conway have been so poor ever since, that when a stranger happens to bring a sovereign into that harp-shaped town they have to send across the water to Llansantffraid for change. So when the tearful prisoner at last said to Pergrin, "If thou wilt let me go, Pergrin, I will give thee three shouts in the time of thy greatest need," he accepted her offer. Carrying her down to the strand of the sea, he put her in the water, and she immediately plunged into the depths.

Days and weeks passed without Pergrin seeing her after this. But one fine hot afternoon he was out fishing in his boat, and many of the fishermen were similarly engaged. The sea was calm, and there was hardly a cloud in the sky, so that no one had any thought of danger. Suddenly the mermaiden emerged out of the blue, sunlit water and shouted in a loud voice, "Pergrin, Pergrin, Pergrin, take up thy net, take up thy net, take up thy net." Pergrin instantly obeyed, drew in his net with great haste, and rowed over the bar homewards, amid the jeers of all the others. By the time he had reached the Pwll Cam a dread storm overspread the sea: the wind blew great guns and the waves ran mountain high. Pergrin reached dry land safely, but all the other fishermen, eighteen in number, found watery graves.

The Cave of the Young Men of Snowdonia

COUNTLESS as were the warriors of Arthur in the cave of Craig y Dinas, there is yet another army of them sleeping in Snowdonia.

Their resting-place is in the steep cliff which is on the left-hand side near the top of Llyn Llydaw. This is how it was discovered. A sheep fell down to a shelf in this precipice, and the Cwm Dyli shepherd, who was a famous climber, with infinite trouble made his way to the spot to rescue the animal. To his astonishment he found there an opening into the rock, only partially hidden by loose stones and turf. He cleared these away, and saw a vast cave stretching into the bowels of the mountain. There was a bright light within; he looked in and saw a host of warriors without number, all asleep, with white hazel wands in their hands. He watched for a long time to see if they would show any signs of waking, but none stirred. Seeing that they were so fast asleep, he felt a great desire to enter the cave and explore it. But as he was squeezing in he struck his head against a bell suspended just above the entrance inside. It rang so that every corner of the immense cavern rang again. All the warriors woke up, and, springing to their feet, gave forth a terrific shout. This so frightened the shepherd that he made off as quickly as he could, and nearly broke his neck on his way down the face of the precipice. From that time he never enjoyed a day's health, and he died before his time. Nobody has since dared as much as to approach the mouth of the Cave of the Young Men of Snowdonia.

Einion and the Fair Family

ONCE on a time a shepherd went up a mountain to look after his sheep. A thick mist came on, and he lost his way, and walked backwards and forwards for many a long hour. At last he got into a low rushy place, where he saw before him many circular rings. He knew at once that they were the circles in which the Fair Family danced, and remembering how many a shepherd who had chanced on these rings had disappeared from mortal eyes, he determined to run away as fast as he could. As he was racing off he was met by an old fat little man. "Stop," said the old man, and there was something in this voice which made Einion (that was the shepherd's name) obey. "What art thou doing?" "I am running home," said the shepherd. "Come after me," said the old man, "and do not utter a word until I bid thee." The shepherd could not choose but obey, and he followed his guide on and on until they came to an oval stone. The old man tapped the stone three times with his walking stick, and the stone rose of its own accord, disclosing a narrow passage leading into the earth. "Follow me fearlessly," said the fat man; "no harm will be done thee." On the youth went, as reluctantly as a dog to be hanged. It was dark in the passage, though a sort of whitish light radiated from the stones which formed the roof: at last the tunnel opened into a fine wooded fertile country. Birds sang in the groves, and streams of clear water, flowing through meadows carpeted with bright flowers, made music as sweet as that of the feathered tribe. Dotting the landscape were splendid mansions, and into one of these Einion was led by the little man.

Both sat down to eat at a table of silver: golden dishes containing the most delicious meats and golden goblets full of exquisite wine came to their places of themselves and disappeared of themselves when done with. This puzzled the shepherd beyond measure: moreover, he heard people talking together around him, but for the life of him he could see no one but his aged friend. At length the fat man said to him, "Thou canst now talk as much as it may please thee." Einion tried to speak, but he found that his tongue would no more stir than if it had been a lump of ice. Three beautiful maidens came in: they looked archly at him and began to talk to him, but still his tongue would not wag. Then one of the maidens came to him, and playing with his fair curling hair, gave him a kiss on his ruddy lips. This loosened the string that bound his tongue, and Einion began to talk freely, and he had much to say, especially to the maiden who had kissed him.

He remained a year and a day with the little man and his daughters without knowing that he had passed more than a day among them, for he was so happy. But by-and-by he began to feel somewhat of a longing to visit his old home, and he asked his fat host if he might go. "Stay a little yet," said he, "and thou shalt go for a while." He asked a second time after some while, and was again refused permission. Mererid (that was what the damsel who kissed him was called) looked very sad when he talked of going away; nor was he himself without feeling a sort of a cold thrill passing through him at the thought of leaving her. The longing for home, however, would not leave him, and he asked a third time to be allowed to go to earth. This time, on condition that he returned on the first night of the new moon, he obtained leave to go.

Everyone was delighted to see him, for it was thought that he had been killed. Another shepherd had been suspected of murdering him, and had been compelled to run away to Merthyr Tydfil (that was where all persons fled to at that time when they wished to avoid punishment) lest he should be hanged. Einion would not tell anyone where he had been, and on the appointed night he went back to Fairyland. Mererid was rejoiced at his return, and before long the twain were wedded, and lived very happily. Einion, however, could not rest contented with his life in Fairyland, and entreated the old man for leave to take his wife with him and dwell on earth. At last the old man consented and gave him much silver and gold, and many precious gems to take with them. So Einion and his bride set out on two ponies whiter than snow and arrived at his old home. With the treasure which they had brought with them they acquired an immense estate, and no couple in the country were more honoured than they. But it was not long before people began to inquire about the pedigree of Einion's wife, and as he would not tell them who she was, they came to the conclusion that she was one of the Fair Family. "Certainly," said Einion, when asked whether this were so, "there can be no doubt that she comes from a very fair family: for she has two sisters who are almost as fair as she is, and if you saw them together, you would admit that this name is a most fitting one."

St. Collen and the King of Faery

ST. COLLEN was so distressed with the wickedness of the people that he withdrew to a mountain and made himself a cell under the shelter of a rock in a remote and secluded spot.

One day when he was in his cell he heard two men conversing about Gwyn ab Nudd, and saying that he was King of Annwn and of the fairies. Collen put his head out of the cell and said to them, "Hold your tongues quickly, those are but Devils." "Hold thou thy tongue," said they, "thou shalt receive a reproof from him." And Collen shut his cell as before. Soon after he heard a knocking at the door of his cell, and someone inquired if he were within. Then said Collen: "I am. Who is it that asks?" "It is I, a messenger from Gwyn ab Nudd, King of Annwn and of the fairies, to command thee to go and speak with him on the top of the hill at noon."

But Collen did not go. And the next day behold the same messenger came, ordering Collen to go and speak with the King on the top of the hill at noon.

But Collen did not go. And the third day behold the same messenger came, ordering Collen to go and speak with the King on the top of the hill at noon. "And if thou dost not go, Collen, thou wilt be the worse for it."

Then Collen, being afraid, arose and prepared some holy water, and put it in a flask at his side and went to the top of the hill. And when he came there he saw the fairest castle he had ever beheld, and around it the best appointed troops, and numbers of minstrels, and every kind of music of voice and instrument, and steeds with youths upon them the comeliest in the world, and maidens of elegant aspect, sprightly, light of foot, of graceful apparel and in the bloom of youth: and every magnificence becoming the court of a great king. A courteous man on the top of the castle bade him enter, saying that the King was waiting for him to come to meat. Collen went into the castle, and when he entered the King was sitting in a golden chair. He welcomed Collen honourably, and desired him to eat, assuring him that besides what he saw he should have the most luxurious of every dainty and delicacy that the mind could desire, and should be supplied with every drink and liquor that his heart could wish: and that there should be in readiness for him every luxury of courtesy and service, of banquet and of honourable entertainment, of rank and of presents: and every respect and welcome due to a man of wisdom. "I will not eat," said Collen.

"Didst thou ever see men of better equipment than those in red and blue?" asked the King.

"Their equipment is good enough," said Collen, "for such equipment as it is."

"What kind of equipment is that?" said the King. Then said Collen: "The red on the one part signifies burning, and the blue on the other signifies coldness." With that Collen drew out his flask, and threw the holy water on their heads, whereupon they vanished from his sight, so that there was neither castle, nor troops, nor men, nor maidens, nor music, nor song, nor steeds, nor youths, nor banquet, nor the appearance of anything whatever but the green hillock.

Helig's Hollow

MANY ages ago, the fair and fertile tract of country stretching from the Gogarth (better known as the Great Orme) to Bangor, and from Llanfair Fechan to Ynys Seiriol (Puffin Island is another and uglier name for this seagirt knoll), was ruled by Helig ab Glannach, and was called Tyno Helig, or Helig's Hollow.

Helig had a daughter, Gwendud: she was as fair as Gwenhwyfar, the wife of Arthur, "when she appeared loveliest at the Offering on the day of the Nativity, or at the feast of Easter," but she had an evil heart, full of wickedness, cruelty and deceit.

She was loved and wooed by the son of one of the barons of Snowdon, and she loved him in return as much as she was capable of loving anyone other than Gwendud, the daughter of Helig. But she would not wed him because he had no golden collar.

Tathal (that was her suitor's name) tried for a long time to win this distinction fairly, but failed. Gwendud would not change her mind, so he determined to procure a collar by foul means.

Rhun, the son of Maelgwn Gwynedd, had led an expedition into Strath Clyde, and after burning and slaying had brought back many prisoners to Caer Rhun, where he held them to ransom. The first captive whose liberty was bought by his kinsmen was a young chieftain who had won a golden collar in the wars against the Picts. Tathal went to him and offered his services as guide. After conducting him through the Perfeddwlad, he treacherously stabbed him and brought back his golden collar.

His story was that they had been set upon by a band of robbers, headed by an outlaw noble, whom he had slain in fair fight. Gwendud now consented to wed him, and Tyno made a great feast, bidding to it all his own kinsmen and those of the bridegroom.

A harper from Bangor was summoned to make music for the revel. The harper had the gift of second sight, and he asked the cupbearer to tell him if he saw anything out of the common when he went down to the cellar to draw the mead. The night was yet young when the cupbearer came in terror to the harper and said: "A stream of water is flowing into the cellar, and hundreds of little fishes are swimming in it."

"Let us fly for our lives," said the harper. The twain fled through the darkness towards the mountains. They were hardly out of the banqueting hall when they heard the sullen roar of a great flood. Soon they heard shrieks of terror, which made the blood run cold in their veins. Looking back they could dimly see the foam of mighty breakers racing towards them. Soon the water was lapping at their heels, and though they ran until their hearts almost burst within their bodies, they were more than once nearly overwhelmed by the vengeful deluge. At last they reached Rhiwgyfylchi, breathless and exhausted with fatigue, and there, safe from the pursuing waves, they waited for the morning. When the sun rose it disclosed an expanse of rippling water where Helig's Hollow had been. Nor has the sea ever given up its conquest.

Some men of Conway have, while fishing on July days when the water is very calm, seen the ruins of Helig's Palace deep down below the surface, but the sight is unlucky, for every man who has espied the drowned walls and towers has died very soon after.

Owen Goes A-wooing

OWEN, one of the men-servants at Nannau, was going to see his sweetheart, who was a milkmaid at Dol y Clochydd. The night was very dark, and Owen lost his way. After wandering about for some time he fell into Llyn Cynnwch. He could not swim, and the water closed over him, and he sank down, down, down. As he descended his brain began to clear, and he found that the process of sinking was by no means as unpleasant as might have been expected. He breathed as freely as on land, and the further he went the clearer became the water. At last he alighted on a level spot at the bottom of the lake. He was surprised to find a beautiful country, with green fields and flowery hedges and leafy trees. Presently a short, fat old man came to him and asked him where he had come from. Owen explained how he had fallen into the lake on his way to see Siwsi, his sweetheart. "You are welcome," said the short, fat old man, and he conducted him to a beautiful mansion where there was a large company assembled, amusing themselves with all kinds of merriment and frolicking.

After he had been there for about an hour or two he went to the short, fat old man and said to him, "Would you be so kind, sir, as to show me the way to Dol y Clochydd? I am late as it is, and I am afraid Siwsi will give me up and go to bed unless I turn up soon." His host tried to induce him to stay, but Owen was anxious to go, and at last his petition was granted. The short, fat old man took him along a level path, which led right underneath the hearthstone of Dol y Clochydd. The stone lifted itself up when Owen came to it, and he found himself in the kitchen. Siwsi was sitting by the fire weeping for him. She was terribly frightened when she saw him, and he had much difficulty in proving to her that he was not a ghost, for instead of being an hour or two late, as he had imagined, he had been missing for over a month.

The Fairy Reward

IANTO LLYWELYN lived by himself in a cottage at Llanfihangel. One night after he had gone to bed he heard a noise outside the door of the house. He opened his window and said, "Who is there? And what do you want?" He was answered by a small silvery voice, "It is room we want to dress our children." Ianto went down and opened the door: a dozen small beings entered carrying tiny babies in their arms, and began to search for an earthen pitcher with water; they remained in the cottage for some hours, washing the infants and adorning themselves. Just before the cock crew in the morning they went away, leaving some money on the hearth as a reward for the kindness they had received.

After this Ianto used to keep his fire of coal balls burning all night long, leaving a vessel of water on the hearth, and bread with its accompaniments on the table, taking care, also, to remove everything made of iron before going to bed. The fairies often visited his cottage at night, and after each visit he found money left for him on the hearth. Ianto gave up working, and lived very comfortably on the money which he received in return for his hospitality from the Fair Family. His income from this source was more than enough to keep himself in comfort, so Ianto married a wife.

Betsi—that was the name of her whom Ianto thus honoured—did not bother about the way in which he got his money before she married him, but after the knot had been tied she became very curious. Ianto refused to tell her, and this of course made her more inquisitive than ever. "I don't believe you get it honestly," she said. Ianto denied by wood, field and mountain that there was anything dishonest about his means of livelihood. She gave him no peace, however. "Nine shames on you," she said, "for having a bad secret from your own dear wife." "But," remonstrated Ianto, "if I tell you, Betsi *bach,* I'll never get any more money." "Ah," she said (she had already had her doubts about Ianto's nightly preparations of fire and hot water), "then it's the fairies." "Drato," said he, "yes, the fairies it is." With that he thrust his hands down in his breeches pocket in a sullen manner and left the house. He had seven shillings in his pockets up to that minute. When he went feeling for them, thinking that a glass of beer and a pipe of tobacco at the inn would not be amiss after such a matrimonial squabble, he found they were gone. In place of them were some pieces of paper, no good even to light his pipe. From that day the fairies brought him no more money, and he had once more to eat his bread in the sweat of his face, which is a more scriptural but less pleasant method of earning a living than gathering up fairy money.

Why Deunant Has the Front Door in the Back

THE cattle of the farmer living at Deunant, close to Aberdaron, were grievously afflicted with the "short disease," which is the malady known in English as the black quarter. Naturally, he thought they were bewitched. Old Beti'r Bont, whose character was by no means above suspicion—she was thought to earn her living by stealing babies for the fairies—had called at Deunant when they were feathering geese and had begged much for one, but she had been refused, and the farmer concluded she was taking her revenge by harassing his stock. So he went to old Beti and told her that he would tie her hands and feet and throw her into a river unless she removed the charm. She vehemently denied possessing any magical powers, and repeated the Lord's Prayer correctly in proof of her innocence. The farmer was not altogether convinced even by this, and made her say, "Rhad Duw ar y da," "God's blessing be on the cattle." Now, if this is spoken over bewitched animals, they are always freed from their disease, but the farmer's stock was no better even after this invocation, and he was at his wits' end.

One night before going to bed he was standing a few steps in front of his house, meditating over his trouble. "I cannot imagine why the cattle do not get better," said he out loud to himself. "I will tell you," said a squeaky little voice close by him. The farmer turned in the direction of the sound and saw a tiny little man, looking very angrily at him. "It is," continued the mannikin, "because your family keeps on annoying mine so much." "How is that?" asked the farmer, surprised and puzzled. "They are always throwing the slops from your house down the chimney of my house," said the little man. "That cannot be," retorted the farmer, "there is no house within a mile of mine." "Put your foot on mine," said the small stranger, "and you will see that what I say is true." The farmer complying, put his foot on the other's foot, and he could clearly see that all the slops thrown out of his house went down the chimney on the other's house which stood far below in a street he had never seen before. Directly he took his foot off the other's, however, there was no sign of house or chimney. "Well, indeed, I am very sorry," said the farmer. "What can I do to make up for the annoyance which my family has caused you?" The tiny little man was satisfied by the farmer's apology, and he said:

"You had better wall up the door on this side of your house and make another in the other side. If you do that, your slops will no longer be a nuisance to my family and myself." Having said this he vanished in the dusk of the night.

The farmer obeyed, and his cattle recovered. Ever after he was a most prosperous man, and nobody was so successful as he in rearing stock in all Lleyn. Unless they have pulled it down to build a new one, you can see his house with the front door in the back.

Getting Rid of the Fairies

NOT so very far from the caves of Ystrad Fellte, in Breconshire, is a farmhouse called Pen Fathor, which in the olden time was inhabited by Morgan Rhys and his family. They were well-to-do and ought to have been happy, but they were sorely troubled by the fairies. This was owing to an insult which was unwittingly offered to one of them. Morgan's wife, Modlen, seeing a little fairy lady poorly clad, had, in the kindness of her heart, given her a gown. She was furiously angry and tore it to shreds. (Not that the Fair Family are always offended by such proffered gifts. A shepherd of Cwm Dyli used to spend the summer with his sheep on the mountain. Waking up one morning in his hut he saw a little fairy mother washing a baby close to his bed, and he noticed that she had scarcely anything wherewith to clothe the shivering little creature. Stretching out his arm to reach a ragged old shirt, he threw it to her, saying, "Take that, poor thing, and wrap it around him." She took the shirt thankfully, old as it was, and departed. Every evening after this, as regularly as clockwork, the shepherd found a silver coin in an old clog in his hut, and this lasted for many years.) After this the Fair Family gave Morgan and his household no peace. When they were in the kitchen there were all manner of noises in the cowhouse (in those days it was on the same floor as the kitchen, and only separated by a rhag-ddor, or a half-door). When they went to the cowhouse everything was upset in the kitchen. When they were at their meals, dust was shaken into their food through the crevices of the flooring above. At night their crockery was broken, their cows were milked dry, and their horses ridden until their wind was broken.

The nuisance was unbearable, and Morgan consulted a wise woman at Penderyn as to the best means of ridding Pen Fathor of such troublesome company. She must have been a pretender and no real wise woman, for though her directions were faithfully carried out, they ended in nothing but disappointment and expense. "You must make out," she said, "that you are going to quit your farm for another holding in Ystrad Towy. Collect all your stock together, and put the whole of your household goods upon wagons. Then go down to Pont Nedd Fechan, as if you meant to leave Ystrad Fellte for ever. You can then return through Hirwain and Penderyn, and you will find that the fairies have deserted your house, for it is their invariable custom to quit a place which passes from an old family into new hands."

This Morgan did, and the procession had got as far as Pont Nedd Fechan when Morgan was accosted by an old neighbour whom he met. "And so you are going to leave us, Morgan *bach*, are you?" Before Morgan had time to reply, a thin soprano voice piped out of a churn upon the top of one of the wagons, "Yes, we are going to live in Ystrad Towy." The scheme had failed, and there was nothing to do but to return by the same way that they had come by. The behaviour of the fairies was more outrageous than ever after this. They even tried to steal Modlen's baby from her arms in bed one night. But she screamed and held on, and as she afterwards told the neighbours, "God and me were too hard for them."

Then Morgan consulted a cunning man of great reputation living at Pentre Felin, and his plan was crowned with success. It was the commencement of the oat harvest, when the Cae Mawr, or big field, by the river side, which it took fifteen men to mow in a day, was ripe for the sickle. "How many of the neighbours will be coming to help us with the Cae Mawr to-morrow?" asked Modlen in a loud voice, so that the fairies might hear. "There will be fifteen of us in all," answered Morgan, "and you must see that the food is substantial and sufficient for the hard job before us." "The fifteen men will have no reason to complain about that," said Modlen, "they shall be fed according to our means."

Next morning, when the fifteen men were showing their prowess in the big field, Modlen set about preparing food for the mowers. She procured a sparrow, trussed it like a fowl, and roasted it before the kitchen fire. She then placed some salt in a nutshell, and set the sparrow and a piece of bread no bigger than her fist upon the table. She had just taken the horn to summon the mowers to dinner when the fairies, beholding the scanty provision made for the midday meal of so many hungry men, said, "We have lived long: we were born just after the earth was made, but never have we beheld a sight like this. Let us quickly depart from this place, for the means of our hosts are exhausted. Who before this was ever so poor as to serve up just one sparrow as the dinner of fifteen mowers?" They departed that very night, and Pen Fathor was never troubled by them afterwards.

The Mantle of Kings' Beards

THERE were formerly two kings in Britain named Nynio and Peibio. One moonlight night, as they were walking the fields, "See," said Nynio, "what a beautiful and extensive field I possess." "Where is it?" said Peibio. "There it is," said Nynio, "the whole sky, as far as vision can extend." "And dost thou see," said Peibio, "what countless herds and flocks of cattle and sheep I have grazing in thy field?" "Where are they?" said Nynio. "There they are," said Peibio, "the whole host of stars which thou seest, each of golden brightness, with the Moon for their shepherdess, to look after their wanderings." "They shall not graze in my pasture," said Nynio. "They shall," said Peibio. "They shall not," said the one. "They shall," said the other. From contention it came to furious war, and the armies and subjects of both the kings were nearly all destroyed.

Rhitta Gawr, King of Wales, hearing of the desolation wrought by these mad monarchs, determined to attack them. Having previously consulted the laws and his people, he marched against them, vanquished them and cut off their beards. When the other Kings of Britain, twenty-eight in number, heard of this, they combined all their legions to avenge the degradation committed on the two disbearded kings, and made a fierce onset on Rhitta the Giant and his forces; and furiously bold was the engagement. But Rhitta won the day. "This is my extensive field," said he then, and he shaved the beards of these kings also, so that he now had the beards of thirty Kings of Britain.

When the kings of the surrounding countries heard of the

disgrace inflicted on all these disbearded kings, they armed themselves against Rhitta and his men, and tremendous was the conflict. But Rhitta achieved a decisive victory, and then exclaimed, "This is my immense field," and at once ordered his men to shave off the beards of the kings. Then pointing to them, "These," said he, "are the animals that grazed my field, but I have driven them out: they shall no longer depasture there!" After that he took up all the beards and trimmed with them a mantle for himself that extended from head to heel: and Rhitta was twice as large as any other person ever seen.

Then Rhitta sent a messenger to the Court of King Arthur to say that he had trimmed a mantle with kings' beards, and to command Arthur carefully to flay off his beard and send it to him. Out of respect to his preeminence over other kings his beard should have the honour of the principal place. But if he refused to do it, he challenged him to a duel, with this offer, that the conqueror should have the mantle and the beard of the vanquished. Then was Arthur furiously wroth and said:

"Were it permitted to slay a messenger, thou shouldest not go back to thy lord alive, for this is the most arrogant and villainous message that ever man sent to a king. By the faith of my body, Rhitta shall lose his head."

Arthur gathered his host and marched into Gwynedd and encountered Rhitta. The twain fought on foot, and they gave one another blows so fierce, so frequent and so powerful, that their helmets were pierced and their skullcaps were broken and their arms were shattered and the light of their eyes was darkened by sweat and blood. At the last Arthur became enraged, and he called to him all his strength: and boldly angry and swiftly resolute and furiously determined, he lifted up his sword and struck Rhitta on the crown of the head a blow so fiercely-wounding, severely-venomous and sternly-smiting that it cut through all his head armour and his skin and his flesh and clove him in twain. And Rhitta gave up the ghost, and was buried on the top of the highest mountain of Eryri, and each of his soldiers placed a stone on his tomb. The place was afterwards known as Gwyddfa Rhitta, Rhitta's Barrow, but the English call it Snowdon.

Pedws Ffowk and St. Elian's Well

PEDWS FFOWK was for three years afflicted with a complaint which nobody could understand. She was well and yet she was not well: she was sick and yet she was not sick. That is to say, she had no ache or pain, and her appetite was good. But all the time she became thinner and thinner, until at last she was nothing but skin and bone. She went to doctor after doctor, but they could not find out what was the matter with her. She consulted quacks also, but even they did her no good. Finally, she went to a wise man. He, after hearing her story, said, "Someone has put you into St. Elian's Well."

"What do you mean by that?" asked Pedws.

"Someone has gone to the woman who keeps the well," answered the wise man, "and put your name on the register, and thrown a pin into the well, together with a pebble with your initials on it."

"Well, what is the harm of that?" inquired Pedws, who had not heard of the power of the cursing well.

"You are cursed," was the reply, "and unless the curse is removed, you will pine away and die."

"But what am I to do?" said Pedws, now thoroughly frightened.

"You must go to the woman who keeps the well, and pay her to take you out of the well," was the wise man's advice.

Pedws lost no time in going to the guardian of the well, who, for a small fee, agreed to examine her register. Sure enough, the name of Pedws Ffowk was there inscribed, and the date of the entry corresponded with the time when she had begun to waste away. On the payment of another and a larger sum of money the priestess of the fountain agreed to take out of the water the stone on which the initials of Pedws Ffowk were scratched. From that moment flesh began to grow on her bones, and before long her clothes, which had hung upon her like rags upon a scarecrow, were filled out as well as they had ever been. Pedws lived to a good old age, and her greatest trouble was that she never found out which of her best friends had put her into the well.

Magic Music

THERE was once a pious monk at Clynnog Fawr, in Arfon, whose delight was in the law of the Lord, and in His law did he meditate day and night. One evening he was walking in deep thought through a grove near the monastery, by the side of a stream, which tumbled noisily over the stones in its hurry to reach the sea. Suddenly a bird burst into song, and its lay was the sweetest and most lovely music that the man of God had ever listened to. He paused to listen, and remained listening until the bird ceased to pour forth its golden notes. Then he passed out of the grove and looked around. The monastery was unchanged, but everything else was different. He went to the monastery. The faces of all the monks were strange to him, and not a soul knew him. The brethren crowded round him, and he told them how he had been listening in the grove for a short time to the melody of a bird. He asked them to put him in a cell, for he wanted to pray. This was done. Some time after a brother went to see whether he could render him any service. The cell was empty, but there was a handful of ashes on the stone floor.

Search was made in the books of the monastery, and it was found that some hundreds of years before a brother had gone out of the monastery and never returned. Since then the trees in which he listened to the magic music have been called the Grove of Heaven.

Sili go Dwt

At Nant Corfan, in Cwm Tafolog, in Montgomeryshire, there once lived a poor woman who had been left a widow, with a little baby. "Whosoever hath, to him shall be given, and he shall have more abundance; but whosoever hath not, from him shall be taken away even that he hath." This was the case with the poor widow, for the Gwylliaid Cochion, the Red Banditti, of Mawddwy, sent one of their number down her chimney, although she had put scythes in it to prevent such an entry, and robbed her of all the money which she had put by to pay the rent. Not content with that, they drove away all her cattle to their lairs.

The poor woman was weeping as if her heart would break, when suddenly there came a knock at the door, and a tall old lady, dressed in green, came in with a long staff in her hand. "Why are you weeping?" asked the green lady. And the widow told her of her great misfortunes.

"Be comforted," said the stranger, "for I have gold here more than enough to pay your rent and to buy cattle to replace those which these wicked robbers have taken away." With that she brought out a great bag from under her cloak, and poured out a great heap of yellow gold on the little round table by the fire. The widow's eyes glistened and her mouth watered at the sight. "All this will I give you," said the green lady, "if you will give me what I ask for." "I will give you anything I have in my possession," said the widow; her belongings were so few that the best of them, she thought, would be a very poor exchange for the gold which was gleaming bright in the light of the peat fire. "I am not unreasonable," said the green lady, "and I always like to do a good turn for a small reward. All I ask is that little boy lying in the cradle there."

The widow felt as if she had been stabbed to the heart, and she begged and prayed the fairy (for such, it was now clear, she was) to take anything rather than her little boy. "No," said the fairy, "you must let me have your baby. I cannot by the law we live under take him until the third day. I will come back with the gold the day after to-morrow, and if you want the gold you know the condition. But stay, if you can then tell me my right name I will not take your boy." With that she gathered up the yellow metal into her bag and went out.

The poor widow was more wretched than ever. Much as she longed for the fairy's money, she loved her little son more than all the gold on earth, and the very thought of losing him kept her from sleeping all night. The next day she went to some relatives at Llanbrynmair to see whether they could help her in her trouble, but though they had the heart they had not the means to succour her, and she had to return empty-handed. As she was going through a wood she saw an open space among the trees, and in the middle of it was a fairy ring. A little woman was dancing wildly round this ring by herself and singing. The widow could not hear the words of the song from where she was, so she crept as silently as a mouse within hearing distance. Then she heard:

"How the widow would laugh if she was aware
That Sili go Dwt is the name that I bear."

When the widow heard this she felt as if a ton weight had been lifted off her heart: she stole away as noiselessly as she had approached, and made for home as fast as her legs would carry her.

The next day the fairy came again, as she had said, in the guise of a tall old lady as before, dressed in green and with a long staff in her hand. She poured the gold on the little table by the fire once more, and said that the widow could have it if she either gave up her baby or guessed her name. The widow thought that she would have some sport with the fairy, and she asked: "How many guesses will you give me?" "As many as you like," said the fairy. Then the widow tried every strange name that she had ever heard of, all the English names she remembered, and old Welsh names like Garmy, Gorasgwrn, Rhelemon, Enrydreg, Creiddylad, Ellylw, Gwaedan, Rathtyeu, Corth, Tybiau, Cywyllog, Peithian. But the fairy shook her head at each. Then the widow said, "I will have one more guess. Is your name Sili go Dwt, by any chance?" The fairy went up the chimney in a blaze of fire, such was her rage and disappointment. With the gold she left behind her the widow paid the rent and bought cattle, and there was enough to fill an old stocking besides.

She lived happily ever afterwards, and the boy, when he grew up, had the satisfaction of helping Baron Owen to hang a few dozens of the Red Banditti, who had robbed his mother, on the trees of their forest lair.

Another Changeling

ONE wet, cold, stormy summer in the olden time a baby was born at Dyffryn Mymbyr, near Capel Curig. The homestead was so far from any church, and the rain had made the roads so impassable, that the parents did not take the child to be baptised, in the hope of getting finer weather and drier roads. Then the hay harvest came: on the few days when it was fine all the family were of course hard at work in the fields, trying to save the harvest, and no one could be spared to take the baby to the parson: on the other days it rained old women and sticks, and no one could stir out of the house.

After a downpour lasting a week there came a beautifully fine day, and all who could handle a rake went to the fields to turn the sodden and blackening hay to be dried by sun and wind. The baby was left sleeping in its cradle in the house under the charge of its grandmother, who was so old and feeble that it was with difficulty that she could move even from one side of the house to the other. She sat in a great straw chair by the side of the fire, and under the genial influence of the heat thrown out by the burning peat she first of all blinked and nodded, and then fell fast asleep with her chin on her breast.

As she slumbered, who should come into the house but a troop of the Fair Family. They took the unbaptised baby out of its cradle and put in its stead one of their own cross-grained, peevish infants. It at once began to whine and whimper, and the noise it made awakened the sleeping granny. She hobbled to the cradle, and instead of the plump, good-tempered baby which had been lying there, she found a thin, wizened thing with an old man's face, tossing about and crying as loudly as its lungs would permit. "This is a changeling," she at once said to herself; "that old family has been here while I slept."

She took the dinner horn and blew it to call the mother home. She came without delay, and hearing the crying did not pause to ask the grandmother why she had been summoned, but went at once to the cradle and lifted up the little one without looking at him. She hugged him, she tossed him up and down, she sang lullaby to him, but nothing was of any avail: he continued without stopping to scream enough to break her heart, and she did not know what to do to calm him. At last she looked at him: she saw at once that he was not her own dear little boy. She looked again, and his ugliness made her feel quite ill. She gave up the attempt to quiet him, and putting him back in the cradle, let him cry to his heart's content. "This is not my baby," she said. "No, it certainly is not," replied the grandmother. "I fell asleep for a little while, and the fairies must have taken away your boy while I slept, putting this ill-tempered brat in his place."

The whole family was now summoned from the hayfield, and an anxious consultation took place. It was resolved that the father should go to the parson of Trawsfynydd—there was no one skilled in such matters nearer—to ask him what to do. Off he tramped the next day, and right glad he was to get away from the "cold" screaming of the changeling, which had never ceased from the time he came to Dyffryn Mymbyr. The parson was reluctant to advise at first, on the ground that it served the parents right for not having the baby baptised: an unbaptised child, he said, was almost certain to be changed by the fairies. But the father's explanation appeased him, and he counselled thus: "There are many ways," he said, "of getting rid of a fairy changeling. One is to leave it all night in a cradle under an oak tree. Many mothers have had their own babies restored to them in this way. Another way is to throw the changeling into a river or lake. There was once a couple at Corwrion to whom twin children were born. The fairies stole them, and left two of their own brats instead. The mother took them to a wooden bridge and dropped them into the river beneath. Before they reached the water the old elves of the blue trousers caught them, and when the woman returned to her house she found her own children back again. I have also known changelings got rid of by throwing iron at them. But the best plan is this: take a shovel and cover it with salt, and make the figure of the cross in the salt. Then take the shovel to the room where the changeling is lying: open the window, and place the shovel on the fire until the salt is burnt. Then you will get your child back again."

As soon as he got home the father did as the parson directed. When the shovel was placed on the fire the changeling suddenly ceased its crying, and by the time the salt was hot it had gone away, seen of no one. The door was opened, and there was the lost baby, whole and unscathed, lying on the threshold.

A Fairy Borrowing

THE fairies were in the habit of borrowing things from the old woman of Hafod Rugog. They continually came for her *padell* and *gradell.* (The *gradell* is a sort of round flat iron on which the dough is put: the *padell* is the pan put over it. This method of baking makes beautiful bread.) By way of payment they used to leave money or a loaf in her kitchen at night.

One day she went to her peat stack to get fuel for her fire, and one of the little women came to ask her for her *troell bach,* or wheel, for spinning flax. "I am tired of lending you my things," said the old woman, who was in a bad temper that day, "but you shall have what you want if you grant me two things, that the first thing I put my hand on at the door break, and the first thing I put my hand on in the house be lengthened half a yard."

Now this is why the old crone made these requests: there was a grip stone *(carreg afael),* as it is called, in the wall near the door of her house, and she wanted to break it; and in the house she had a piece of flannel which she wanted to make into a jerkin, but it was half a yard too short. The little woman promised to grant her two demands, and was told to take the *troell.*

The old woman put her creel of peat on her back and started home. As she came near the door she slipped on a stone and nearly twisted her ankle: she put her hand on it to rub it, when the joint broke and she fell on her nose. Dragging herself into the house, she rubbed her injured beak, and it immediately shot out half a yard.

Treasure Seeking

THERE is no end of treasure hidden in the mountains of Wales, but if you are not the person for whom it is intended, you will probably not find it. Even if you do find it, you will not be able to secure it, unless it is destined for you.

There is a store of gold in a hillock near Arenig Lake, and Silvanus Lewis one day took his pickaxe and shovel to find it. No sooner had he commenced to dig in earnest than he heard a terrible, unearthly noise under his feet. The hillock began to rock like a cradle, and the sun clouded over until it became pitch dark. Lightning flashes began to shoot their forked streaks around him and pealing thunders to roar over his head. He dropped his pickaxe and hurried helter-skelter homewards to Cynythog. Before he reached there everything was beautifully calm and serene. But he was so frightened that he never returned to fetch his tools. Many another man has been prevented in the same way from continuing his search.

The farmer of Rhiwen, while helping a sheep that had fallen among the rocks to get to safety, discovered a cave near the Marchlyn Mawr, the Great Horse-lake. He entered and found it full of treasure and arms of great value. He was stretching forth his hand to lift up some of them when the noise of a thousand thunders burst over his head, and the cave became as dark as night. He groped his way out as fast as he could. When he had emerged into the welcome light of the sun, he cast his eye on the lake. It was stirred to its depths, and its white-crested waves dashed through the jagged teeth of the rocks up to the spot on which he stood. As he continued to gaze at the storm, he beheld in the middle of the lake a coracle. In it were three women, the fairest that the eye of man has ever fallen upon, but the dread aspect of him who was rowing them towards the mouth of the cave sent thrills of horror through him. He was able somehow to escape him, but he never enjoyed a day's health after that, and the mere mention of the Marchlyn in his hearing was enough to throw him into pitiable terror.

There is an iron chest full of gold in the subterranean passage which connects Castell Coch with Cardiff. It is guarded by two eagles in a darkness so profound that nothing can be seen but the fire of their sleepless eyes.

Once upon a time a party of stout-hearted Welshmen determined to secure these riches, and took with them pistols loaded with silver bullets which had been blessed by a priest. They penetrated into the tunnel far enough to see the fiery eyes of the guardians of the chest. They fired: the bullets rattled harmlessly on the feathers of the birds. The ground shook under their feet: the eagles attacked them with beak and claw, and they barely escaped with their lives.

A shepherd, wandering about the mountain near Ogwen Lake, chanced to come across the mouth of a cave. He entered and found in it countless vessels of bronze of every shape and description. He tried to lift one up, intending to take it home, but it was too heavy for him to move.

He resolved to go away and to return early on the morrow with friends to help him, but before going he closed the mouth of the cave with stones and sods so as to leave it safe. While he was engaged in this work he remembered having heard how others like him had found caves and failed to rediscover them. He could procure nothing that would satisfy him as a mark, but after puzzling his brains for a long time he hit upon a plan. He took out his knife, and whittled his stick all the way as he went towards his home until he came to a familiar path: the chips were to guide him back to the cave.

This was a cunning device, but it did not succeed. When the morning came the shepherd and his friends set out, but when they reached the spot where the chips should begin, not one was to be seen. They had been every one of them picked up by the fairies, and the shepherd's discovery of the treasure was in vain, because he was not the man for whom it is intended.

It is for a Gwyddel (the home of the Gwyddyl is now Ireland) that the vessels are destined. He will come to the neighbourhood to tend sheep, and one day when he goes up to the mountain, just when fate shall see fit to bring it about, a black sheep with a speckled head will run before him and make straight for the cave; the sheep will go in, with the Gwyddel shepherd in pursuit trying to catch it. On entering he will discover the treasure and take possession of it. (It once belonged to his nation, when the Gwyddyl and the Britons contended for the possession of Snowdonia.)

If you are a boy, and the owner of a white dog with silver eyes (you may not know that every such dog can see the wind), you should lose no time in going to Llangollen. Under Castell Dinas Bran there is a cave which is full of treasure. The dog will lead you to the place, and you will become rich beyond the dreams of avarice.

The Richest Man

IN TIME long past there lived in a certain parish a great and wealthy lord. He had gold and silver, houses and land, and every honour which his country could give him.

One morning, after the cock had crowed three times, he heard a voice proclaiming three times, "This very night shall the richest man in this parish die." He was greatly troubled, and sent his servants in hot haste for the best of physicians far and near. He took to his bed, and the physicians watched unceasingly by his side, administering to him every medicine and every support of life which their study of the healing art had discovered.

The night came and wore away, although it appeared to the nobleman as long as a man's life. The dawn broke, and the nobleman and the physicians rejoiced exceedingly that he was still alive. While they rejoiced, lo, the church bell tolled the knell of someone dead. They sent to enquire who it was. The answer came that it was a poor old blind beggar-man, who was often to be seen sitting more than half-naked at the roadside asking an alms. The nobleman said, "The voice proclaimed that the greatest and richest man in the parish would die. The old beggar must have been a cheat and impostor. As he has neither children nor relatives, to me, the lord of this land, belongs by law the wealth which he must have been possessed of." So he sent his servants to search the hut in which the beggar had died. They found nothing but a truss of straw and a bolster of rushes, with the old man lying dead upon them: there was no food or drink or fire or clothes, and it was seen that the beggar had perished from hunger and cold.

"What then meant the voice?" asked the nobleman. And one of the physicians answered and said, "The blind beggar-man has laid up for himself treasures in Heaven, where neither moth nor rust doth corrupt, and where thieves do not break through and steal. Are these treasures not greater than the uncertain and deceitful riches of this world?"

The nobleman was changed from that hour: he relieved poverty and want, and endowed churches, hospitals and schools. On his death-bed he asked that he should be buried in the beggar-man's grave.

St. Beuno and the Curlew

BOYS who go bird-nesting often wonder why it is so hard to find the nest of the curlew. As a matter of fact it is the fault, as they would consider it, of St. Beuno. When he lived at Clynnog he used to go regularly on Sunday to preach at Llanddwyn, off the coast of Anglesey, walking on the sea with the book of sermons which he used to carry about with him. One Sunday, as he was coming back from Llanddwyn to Clynnog, treading the surface of the sea as if it had been dry land, he dropped his precious writings into the water, and failed to recover them. The saint was much worried, because even for saints the task of writing sermons is a troublesome one.

When he reached dry land he was much relieved to find his book on a stone out of the reach of the tide, with a curlew mounting guard over it. The pious bird had picked it up, and brought it to safety. Thereupon the holy man knelt down and prayed for the protection and favour of the Creator for the curlew. His prayer was heard, and ever since it has been extremely difficult to discover where the long-beaked bird lays its eggs.

The Cat Witches

Huw Llwyd of Cynfael was the seventh son of a family of sons, and therefore he was a conjuror by nature. He increased his knowledge of the black art by the study of magical books, and he ate eagle's flesh, so that his descendants could for nine generations charm for the shingles. (All they had to do was to spit on the rash and say: "Male eagle, female eagle, I send you over nine seas, and over nine mountains, and over nine acres of waste land, where no dog shall bark and no cow shall low, and no eagle shall higher rise"—which is quite simple.)

One night he was supping at an inn in Pentre Voelas. Four men came in and joined him at supper. Now, by his magical skill, Huw Llwyd knew that they were bandits from Yspytty Ifan, and meant to kill him during the night for his money. He made a horn grow out of the centre of the table, and obliged the robbers to gaze at it. He went to bed, and in the morning when he came down the four men were still staring at the horn, as he knew they would be. He departed, leaving them still looking steadily and earnestly at the horn: they were arrested in this position and cast into prison.

Many robberies used to take place at an inn near Bettws-y-Coed. Travellers who put up there for the night were continually relieved of their money, and they could not tell how. They were certain that no one had entered their rooms, because they were found locked in the morning just as they were the night before. Huw Llwyd was consulted, and he promised to unravel the mystery.

He presented himself at the inn one night, and asked for a night's lodging, saying that he was an officer on his way to Ireland. The inn was kept by two sisters: they were both very comely, and made themselves very agreeable to Huw Llwyd at supper. Not to be outdone, he did his best to entertain them with tales of travel in foreign parts which he had never visited. On retiring for the night he said that it was a habit with him to have lights burning in his room all night, and he was supplied with a sufficient quantity of candles to last until the morning. Huw Llwyd made his arrangements for a night of vigil. He placed his clothes on the floor within easy reach of his bed, and his sword, unsheathed, on the bed close to his hand. He secured the door, got into bed, and feigned to sleep. Before long two cats came stealthily down the chimney. They frisked here and there in the room, but the sleeper lay motionless; they chased each other around the bed, and gambolled and romped, but still the sleeper showed no signs of awaking. At last they approached his clothes and played with them, turning them over and over. Ere long the sleeper (who had been very wide awake the whole time) saw one of the cats putting her paw into the pocket which contained his purse. He struck at the thievish paw like lightning with his sword. With a hideous howl both cats disappeared up the chimney, and nothing further was seen of them the whole night.

Next morning only one of the sisters appeared at the breakfast table. Huw Llwyd asked where the other was. Receiving the reply that she was ill and could not come down, he expressed his regret, and proceeded to break his fast. The meal over, "I am now going to resume my journey," he said, "but I must say good-bye to your sister, for I greatly enjoyed her company last night." Many excuses were attempted, but he would not be refused, and at last he was admitted to her presence. After sympathising with her and asking whether he could be of any service, he held out his hand to bid good-bye. The sick lady held out her left hand. "No," said Huw Llwyd laughingly, "I am not going to take your left hand: I have never taken a left hand in my life, and I am not going to begin with yours, white and shapely as it is." Very unwillingly and with evident pain, she put out her right hand. It was swathed in bandages. The mystery was now revealed. The two sisters were witches, and in the form of cats robbed travellers who lodged under their roof: "I have drawn blood from you," said Huw Llwyd, addressing the wounded sister, "and henceforth you will be unable to do any mischief. I will make you equally harmless," he said to the other sister. Seizing her hand, he cut it slightly with a knife, so that the blood came. For the rest of their lives the two sisters were like other women, and no more robberies took place at their inn.

The Swallowed Court

BENLLI, a wicked Prince of Powys, had been married a long time, and he was getting tired of his wife's faded looks and wrinkles. One day, as he was hunting in the Green Forest, a maiden of dazzling beauty rode past him, and he fell in love with her at first sight. He went to the same spot in the forest the next day, and the same vision appeared to him, but vanished before he was able to speak. The third day the damsel appeared again, and he spoke to her, begging her to come and live with him at his palace. "You must put your wife away," said the damsel, "and I will become your wedded wife on one condition. You must allow me to leave you unfollowed one night in every seven, and you must not inquire where I go to or what I do. If you will swear this, and if you do not break your solemn oath whatever happens, my beauty shall know no change until the tall flag-reeds and the long green rushes grow in your hall."

The Prince took a solemn oath to observe this condition, and the Maid of the Green Forest went to live with him at his court. The Prince was spared the necessity of putting his old wife away, because she disappeared before the new bride came to usurp her position. For a long time the Prince lived happily with his young wife, and her beauty seemed to become more and more radiant. He gave her, among other presents, a glorious crown of beryl and sapphire, and a ring with a magnificent diamond worth a king's ransom, and his love was so absorbing that he had no difficulty in abiding by the condition which he had sworn to observe. As time went on, however, the mystery of her absence every seventh night began to oppress him, and he became very unhappy.

About nine years after he had wedded the Maid of the Green Forest he invited, among others, a learned clerk, whose name was Wylan, to a feast. Wylan was skilled in magic, and he noticed that in spite of the splendid banquet with its costly viands and racy wines and mirthful songs, some secret sorrow was brooding over the Prince's mind. Some days after the clerk sought out the Prince and said to him, "Christ save thee, Benlli, what secret sorrow makes thy brow so gloomy?" Then the Prince told him how he had nine years before met the Maid of the Green Forest, and she had become his bride on condition that she should leave him unfollowed one night in every seven. "When the owls and the crickets cry, she leaves my bed and I lie all alone till the day-star appears. Then a heavy slumber falls on my eyelids, and when the sun rises I start from a feverish sleep to find her by my side again. The mystery of it lies heavy on my soul, and I find no peace in the rich banquet, and my whole life is riven with sorrow."

"I can repair thy peace," said clerk Wylan to the troubled Prince, "if thou wilt resign to me the Maid of the Green Forest, and bestow upon the monks of the white Minster a tithe annually of all that feeds in thy palace meadows and all that flows in thy palace vaults."

The prince consented, and clerk Wylan taking with him his clasped book went before midnight to the rocks by the Giant's Grave, and concealed himself by the mouth of a cave leading down to Fairyland. As he lay there a lady hurried past him into the cave. She was royally dressed, and her crown glittered in the moonlight—she was the Maid of the Green Forest.

While she was within the cave the clerk began his potent spells, and he said to the spirits which he summoned, "Let peace be restored to Prince Benlli, for he has promised to the monks of the White Minster a tithe annually of all that feeds in his palace meadows and all that flows in his palace vaults. He has resigned the Maid of the Green Forest to me: let her for ever be as she now appears, and never leave my side. I swear to make her my own at the Cross near the town of the White Minster.

Thither bear her before the break of day, and I will meet and wed her there."

By his magical skill he made these words irrevocable, and departing from the cave's mouth he hastened to the Cross. There he saw a grim ogress smiling and rolling her bleared eyeballs on him. Thin grey hairs stood on her wrinkled chin, and the hair on her head was like the moss of old orchard trees. She stretched out to the clerk a bony finger on which was the ring with the great flashing diamond given by Benlli to the Maid of the Green Forest. "Take me to thy bosom," she said with a hideous laugh, "for I am the wife thou art sworn to wed. A foul ogress am I now, but thirty years agone I was Benlli's blooming bride. But as I lost my beauty I lost his love, and I had recourse to magic.

"On condition of returning to the cave which thou sawest me enter, to be an ogress one night in every seven, I received my youth and beauty again. With these I charmed the Prince anew, for I was the Maid of the Green Forest. I promised him that my beauty should know no change until the tall flag-reeds and the long green rushes grew in his hall. This promise have I kept, for the deep waters have overwhelmed Prince and palace, and the flag-reeds and green rushes already grow in the banqueting chamber. Thy spells, too, were sure, for the peace which thou didst promise doth now bless Benlli, but it is the peace of the dead. Our spells have clashed, and no charm can redress our fate. Take me then to be thy bride, as decreed by oath and spell, and take with me thy reward, a tithe of the pike and dare feeding in the green meadows of the palace and of the water flowing in its vaults." Thus was clerk Wylan caught in his own dark plot.

Llynclys, or Swallowed Court, was the name given to the water which overwhelmed Benlli and his palace. It is on the Welsh border, near Oswestry, and when the surface is smooth, towers and chimneys can be seen at a great depth in the lake. The clerk, who fell into his own trap, is commemorated by the names Croes Wylan, Wylan's Cross, and Tre Wylan, or Wylan's Stead, both near Oswestry.

What Marged Rolant Saw

MARGED ROLANT had a terrible experience once, but luckily she came through it unscathed.

She went from her home in Breconshire to the hiring fair at Rhaiadr Gwy. She was addressed by a very noble-looking gentleman all in black, who asked her if she would be a nursemaid and look after his children. Marged said that she was very fond of children, and inquired what wages she would receive. The sum mentioned by the stranger was so much larger than the usual rate of wages for nursemaids in that part of the country that Marged jumped at the chance offered to her, and the bargain was struck at once.

The stranger said he would like to start home immediately, and fetched a coal-black horse. Marged had to submit to being blindfolded: this done, she mounted behind the stranger and away they rode at a great pace. After some time the horse stopped and the stranger dismounted: he helped Marged to dismount and led her, still blindfolded, for a considerable distance. The handkerchief was then removed, and Marged found herself in a beautiful palace, lighted up by more candles than she could count: many noble-looking ladies and gentlemen were walking about, and a number of little children, as beautiful as angels, came bounding up to her.

The children were put under her charge, and her master gave her a box of ointment to put on their eyes. At the same time he gave her strict orders to wash her hands immediately after using the ointment, and not on any account to let a bit of it touch her own eyes. These injunctions Marged followed strictly, and for some time she was very happy. She sometimes thought, however, that it was odd that the household should always live by candlelight; and she wondered, too, that, grand and beautiful as the palace was, such fine ladies and gentlemen should never leave it. But so it was: no one ever went out but her master.

One morning she thought she would see what would happen if she applied just the teeniest, weeniest bit of ointment to the corner of her eye. Immediately, with the vision of that corner of her eye, she saw herself surrounded by fearful flames: the ladies and gentlemen looked like demons and the beautiful little children resembled hideous imps. Though with the other parts of her eyes she beheld everything as before, she could not help feeling much frightened, but she had enough presence of mind not to show any alarm. However, she took the first opportunity of asking her master's leave to go and see her father and mother. He said she might go, but she must again consent to be blindfolded. Accordingly a handkerchief was put over her eyes: she was again mounted on the coal-black horse behind her master, and was soon put down near her home.

She slept with a Bible under her pillow every night after this, and it was a long time before she ventured to a hiring-fair again.

Ned Puw's Farewell

THE Tal Clegir Cave runs into a long, bare, steep, rugged hill. About its mouth the grass grows thick and rank, and the briars grow undisturbed, tangling and strangling each other.

In the older time it was dangerous to approach within five paces of the *ogof*. Once upon a time a fox, with a pack of hounds in full cry at his tail, was making straight for the entrance: suddenly he turned right round, with his hair all bristled and fretted like frost-work with terror, and ran back into the middle of the pack as if anything earthly, even an earthly death, was preferable to the unearthly horrors of the cave. He escaped, however, for not a dog would go near him, for his hide was all burnished with green, yellow and blue lights, as it were with a profusion of will-o'-the-wisps.

Another time Elias ap Ifan, who for upwards of twenty years had been a drunkard, happened to stagger just upon the rim of the forbidden space and arrived home as sober as a judge, to the amazement of his family. After this Elias was a changed man.

In the twilight of one misty Hallow Eve a shepherd was returning home accompanied by his dog. When he was about a hundred yards from the cave, he heard a faint burst of melody coming from the rocks above the entrance. In a few minutes a figure well known to him became visible. He had a fiddle at his chest, and his legs were on the caper incessantly.

"Ha, ha," said the shepherd, laughing merrily. "Here's old Ned Puw. I remember him wagering that he would dance all the way down the hill and keep up a tune with his fiddle."

Scarcely had he said this, when he noticed to his horror that

Ned had fiddled and capered himself within the fatal five paces. He shouted and shouted to him until the very rocks re-echoed, but Ned Puw seemed perfectly deaf, and fiddled and danced away with all the complacency in the world. The shepherd did not like to abandon him to his fate without making an effort to save him: he ran as near him as he dared, with the intention of pulling him out of the danger zone with his long crook. When he came near him, he saw that by this time Ned's face was as pale as marble, his eyes were staring fixedly and deathfully, and his head was dangling loose and disjointed on his shoulders. He was still fiddling, but his arms seemed to keep the fiddle-stick in motion without the least sympathy from their master. Before the shepherd's very eyes he was, as it were, sucked into the cave by some invisible agency, still fiddling and capering, in the same way as the mist is sucked up by the rising sun in summer. The shepherd was transfixed with terror, and he fancied he could count every hair on the back of his dog that crouched and quivered between his legs, as the cold wind howled mournfully, ploughing up first one hair and then another. Some mysterious power seemed to root him to the spot, and it required a strong effort of will to tear himself away and resume his homeward journey.

On Hallow Eve you can, if you have the courage to approach the entrance of the cave, hear the tune Ned Puw is playing. On certain nights in leap-year you can even see him: a star stands opposite the further end of the cave, enabling you to have a view right through it. There is the wretched fiddler scraping and capering away, and there he will be, for all we know, capering and scraping for ever. A musician who went one Hallow Eve to listen to the strains issuing from the cave took down the tune and named it Ned Puw's Farewell. This is how it goes:

Pennard Castle

PENNARD Castle, in Gower, is now only a few ruined walls all but lost in the sand hills. Once it was the strong castle of a mighty warrior. He was summoned to the aid of a chief of Gwynedd, and his bravery and warlike skill turned the scale against the North Welshman's enemies. As a reward he was given the chief's beautiful daughter in marriage, and on his return to Gower high festival was held to celebrate the victory and the wedding.

At midnight the sentinel pacing round the castle wall thought he heard strange music coming from a grassy plot in the centre of the castle yard. He paused and felt a fear in his heart he could not explain. He called the porter; he also, listening intently, heard the strains. It was a clear moonlight night, and the two, approaching the grassy plot, saw a troop of fairies dancing to the music of little harps. Going into the banqueting hall they told their master that the Fair Family were sporting in the castle. The Lord of the Castle, maddened with wine, ordered his soldiers to drive them away. Then someone said to him, "Have a care: if thou attackest the fairies, it will be thy undoing." The chieftain's rage was unbounded. "What care I," said he, "for man or spirit?" and starting up, he rushed on the moonlit spot, wildly brandishing his sword. But he clove the air in vain, and while he was fruitlessly wielding his weapon, a low voice pronounced his doom. "Since thou hast, without reason, broken in upon our innocent sport, thou shalt be without castle or feast," it said. While the judgment was yet being spoken, a cloud of sand came whirling round the walls, and faster and thicker the storm raged, until walls and towers were overwhelmed. And a mountain of sand was removed from Ireland that night.

The Man with the Green Weeds

LLYN GWERNEN is by the side of the old road leading from Dolgellau to Llanegryn, at the foot of Cader Idris. A number of the farmers of Llanegryn were once hurrying home from a fair at Dolgellau (they were hungry, because the men who sold food at Dolgellau fairs in the olden time used to serve it up so hot that no one could touch it. The farmers were so busy that they could not wait for the dishes to cool, and so it was very little they had for their money). They saw a great man, with green water weeds entwined in his hair, and naked save for a girdle of green weeds, walking round the lake and crying in a querulous tone, "The hour is come but the man is not, the hour is come but the man is not," over and over again.

The farmers were frightened and ran home. Others also who returned home later than they saw and heard him, and it was afterwards found out that the great man with the green water weeds kept on complaining, "The hour is come but the man is not," from ten o'clock at night until five o'clock in the morning.

Some days after the body of an Englishman was found floating, swollen and horrible, on the surface of the lake. He had caused a great stir in the regions round about Cader Idris by sitting all night in the chair in which the astronomer Idris used in early days to watch the stars. (Idris was of more than ordinary stature. One day in walking he felt something in his shoe hurting him; he pulled it off and shook out three stones, which are still to be seen by the Lake of the Three Pebbles, Llyn y Tri Graienyn. One of them is twenty-four feet long, eighteen feet broad, and twelve feet high.) His object was to test the truth of the saying that anyone who spent a night in the chair would by morning be either mad, or a poet, or a corpse. So far from being a poet by the next day, he was not even a bard, and he certainly was not dead then. It was therefore concluded that his intellect was deranged thereby, and he had in this state fallen into the clutches of the man with the green weeds, who had dragged him into the depths of the lake. The objection to that idea was that he must have been mad beforehand, because his chief delight was to climb to the summits of mountains. The folk who dwell at the feet of such mountains as Cader Idris and Snowdon make it a boast that they are much too sensible to attempt anything so silly.

Goronwy Tudor and the Witches of Llanddona

VERY few men in Anglesey in the olden days dared to cross any of the Witches of Llanddona, and those who were bold enough to do so suffered grievously for their rashness. But Goronwy Tudor, who lived not far from Llanddona, was reckless enough to defy even Bella Fawr, Big Bella, the most famous and most dreaded of all the witches of that uncanny village, and he was not a ha'porth the worse.

Perhaps you do not know the history of the Llanddona witches. Long ago a boat came ashore in Red Wharf Bay without rudder or oars, full of men and women half dead with hunger and thirst. In early days it was the custom to put evil-doers in a boat to drift oarless and rudderless on the sea, and when this boat was swept by wind and waves on the beautiful sands of Llanddona, the good people who then lived there prepared to drive it back into the sea, thinking it was manned by criminals. But the strangers caused a spring of pure water to burst forth on the sands (the well still remains, and this decided their fate. They were allowed to stay and to build cottages. But they did not change their evil natures. The men lived by smuggling, and the women begged and practised witchcraft.

It was impossible to overcome the smugglers in a fray, for each of them carried about with him a black fly tied in a knot of his neckerchief. When their strength failed them in the fight they undid the knots of their cravats, and the flies flew at the eyes of their opponents and blinded them. The women used to visit the farmhouses, and when they asked for a pound of butter, a loaf of bread, some potatoes, eggs, a fowl, part of a pig, or what not, they were not denied, because they cursed those who refused them. If they attended a fair or market, no one ventured to bid against them for anything.

But Goronwy Tudor was not afraid of them. He had a birth-mark above his breast, which is a great protection against witch-craft, and he knew how to break nearly every spell. He had the plant which is called Mary's turnip growing in front of his house: he also nailed horseshoes above every door, and put rings made of the mountain ash under the doorposts, thus making his house and all his farm buildings safe. To make them doubly sure he sprinkled earth from the churchyard in all his rooms, and in his byre, stable and pigstye. When the animals were in the fields, however, he had some difficulty in securing them from harm. One day when he went to fetch his cows from the meadow to be milked he found them sitting like cats before a fire, with their hind legs beneath them. Goronwy took the skin of an adder, burnt it and scattered the ashes over the horns of the cows. They got up at once, and walked off with their usual dignity to that byre.

Another day the milk would not turn into butter, and a very unpleasant smell arose from the churn. Goronwy took a crow-bar, heated it red hot, and put it in the milk. Out jumped a large hare, and ran away through the open door of the dairy. After this the milk was churned into beautiful butter.

Some time after the supply of milk began to decline, and the butter made from it was so bad and evil-smelling that the very dogs would not touch it. The milk became scantier and scantier, until at last it ceased altogether, and the cows gave nothing but blood. Goronwy watched in the fields at night and saw a hare going up to a cow and sucking it. She squirted from her mouth and nostrils the milk she had sucked, and then went on to another cow. She did the same with her and with all the other cows. Goronwy knew that it was old Bella in the form of a hare, and he prepared to stop her evil-doing and to punish her. The next night he took his gun, putting into it a silver coin instead of shot (shot cannot penetrate a witch's body), and placed a bit of vervain under the stock. When he saw the hare milking the cows he fired at her. The hare immediately ran off in the direction of

Bella's cottage, with Goronwy after her. He was not so fleet of foot as puss, but he managed to keep her in sight, and saw her jumping over the lower half of the door of the house. Going up to the cottage he heard the sound of dreadful groans. When he reached the door he went in. There was no hare to be seen, but old Bella was sitting by the fire with blood streaming from her legs. He was never again troubled by old Bella in the shape of a hare, and by drawing blood from the bewitched kine he broke the spell.

Bella made one more attempt to injure him. She went to the Cold Well and launched at him the great curse of the Witches of Llanddona:

May he wander for ages many,
And at every step, a stile,
At every stile, a fall;
At every fall, a broken bone,
Not the largest nor the least bone,
But the chief neckbone, every time.

Goronwy felt in his bones that he had been cursed. He got some witch's butter that grows on decayed trees and stuck pins in it. When the pain inflicted by the pins penetrated her body, Bella had willy-nilly to appear before him. She was screaming with pain, and Goronwy refused to take the pins which were causing the anguish out of the butter until she said: "Rhad Duw arnat ti ac ar bopeth ar a feddi—God's blessing on thee and on everything that thou possessest." After this neither Bella nor any of her tribe had any power over Goronwy or his wife, or his man-servant or his maid-servant, or his ox or his ass, or anything that was his.

Robin's Return

Robin Meredydd lived near Pant Sion Siencyn, in Carmarthenshire. As he was going afield early one fine summer's morning he heard a little bird singing very sweetly on a tree close by his path. Allured by the enchanting strain, he sat down under the tree until the music ceased, when he arose and looked about him. What he saw filled him with amazement. The tree which was green and full of life when he sat down was now withered and barkless. He returned to the farmhouse which he had left. It was covered with ivy, and in the doorway stood an old man whom he had never before seen. "What are you doing there?" asked Robin. "That's a pretty question," said the old man, angrily. "Who are you that dare to insult me in my own house?" "In—your—own—house?" repeated Robin. "Yes, certainly," said the old man. "But what is your name?" "I am Robin Meredydd, and it is only a few minutes since I went out of this house and sat under yonder tree to listen to a little bird's song." "Robin *bach,* and is this indeed you?" cried the old man. "I often heard my grandfather, your father, bewail your absence. Long were you searched for, and old Siwan, Pant y Ceubren, said you were under the power of the fairies and would not be released until the last sap of that sycamore tree would be dried up. Come into the house, my dear uncle, I am your nephew." The old man took Robin by the hand, but Robin crumbled into dust on the doorstep.

The Harper's Gratuity

Sion Rhobert was a harper living at Hafod Elwy, in Denbighshire. One evening he went to Llechwedd Llyfn, in the neighbourhood of Cefn Brith, to a merry evening, and it was late before the lads and lasses separated. At last he was allowed to wend his way homeward, and he started walking over the bare mountain. As he came near a lake called Llyn-dau-ychain he saw on its verge a splendid palace, brilliantly illuminated. He was vastly surprised, because he had been many times that way before without observing a dwelling-house of any kind. Seeing, however, is believing, as Sion argued with himself. When he came near he was hailed by a very splendid servant, who invited him to enter. Sion was ushered into a great room, lighted by thousands of candles, and sumptuously furnished. A servant in pale-blue livery handed him a cup filled with sparkling wine, after drinking which Sion felt convinced that he was, without a shadow of a doubt, the best harper that the world had ever seen. The guests surrounded him and, addressing him by name (this Sion considered strange, as he could not remember meeting any of them before), asked him to play. Sion consented, and the company began to dance very spiritedly. When the first dance was over one of the guests took Sion's hat and collected money for him, bringing it back filled with gold and silver. After this Sion kept on playing, and the company continued to dance until the dawn of day, when one by one the guests disappeared, and Sion was left alone. Perceiving a couch, he laid himself thereon, and was soon fast asleep. He did not awake until midday, and then he found himself lying on the heather. The palace had vanished, and the gold and silver in his hat had been converted into withered leaves.

Six and Four Are Ten

A CONJOUROR, on his way to Llanrwst, turned into the tavern at Henllan one evening and called for a glass of beer and some bread and cheese. When he asked for his reckoning, he was charged tenpence—fourpence for the beer and sixpence for the bread and cheese. This charge he considered outrageous, but he did not condescend to dispute it. He determined, however, to have his revenge, and before departing he took a scrap of paper, wrote on it a spell, and put it under the table leg.

The landlord and landlady went to bed early, telling the maidservant to clear away the things which had been set before the conjuror. No sooner were their heads on the pillow than they heard shouting and jumping downstairs. The maid was shrieking at the top of her voice:

"Six and four are ten,
Count it o'er again,"

and dancing wildly. Surprised and angry, they asked her what was the matter, but the only answer they received was:

"Six and four are ten,
Count it o'er again,"

and the girl went on dancing.

The thought now struck the landlord that the dancer had gone out of her mind. He got up and went down to see. The moment he placed his foot in the room he gave a hop, skip and a jump, joined the girl in her mad dance, and with her he shrieked out:

"Six and four are ten,
Count it o'er again,"

The noise was doubled, and if the landlady was surprised and angry before, she was now astounded and furious. She shouted to the scandalous couple to cease their noise, but all to no purpose. They bellowed more loudly than before:

"Six and four are ten,
Count it o'er again,"

and danced still more vigorously.

The landlady could stand it no longer: she left her bed and went downstairs. The sight of her husband and maid shamelessly dancing together and yelling:

"Six and four are ten,
Count it o'er again."

made her wrath overflow, and she determined to put a stop to the proceedings. Seizing a big stick, she bounded into the room, but before she could belabour the heads and shoulders of the two dancers as she had intended, she found herself capering like them and joining in the chorus:

"Six and four are ten,
Count it o'er again,"

The uproar was now great indeed, and the neighbours came to see what was the matter. All who ventured into the room joined in the dance and chorus, and soon the room was full of men and women, leaping and frisking and yelling at the tops of their voices:

"Six and four are ten,
Count it o'er again."

Then one of the spectators, more quick-witted than the rest, remembered that he had seen the conjuror leaving the tavern, and at once guessed that he was responsible for this frantic revel. Hurrying after him, he overtook him on the road to Llanrwst, and begged him to release the people from his spell. The conjuror, chuckling at the humour of the punishment he had meted out, consented. "Take," said he, "the piece of paper which is under the table leg and burn it, and they will then stop their row."

The man ran back as fast as he could, rushed to the table and cast the paper into the fire. Immediately the dancing and shouting ceased, and the performers fell down, panting and exhausted after their exertions.

Envy Burns Itself

TALHAIARN, a learned and wise bard, had a son named Tanwyn, who, when he arrived at man's estate, was desirous of leaving his father's house and seeking his fortune in the world. Talhaiarn said to him, "My son, I have neither gold nor silver to give thee, but I have instructed thee in all useful learning and becoming conduct. There is no need to give thee further counsel except what I now say to thee, namely, 'Pass not by any man who preaches God's word without stopping to listen.'"

After receiving his father's blessing, Tanwyn departed. After travelling a considerable way, he came to a long and even beach by the seaside, and with the point of his staff he wrote on the sand, "Whoso wishes evil to his neighbour, to himself will it come." After he had passed on his way, it chanced that a wealthy and powerful nobleman saw the writing on the sand. He overtook Tanwyn and asked him, "Was it thou that didst write on the sand?" "Yes," answered Tanwyn. "Let me," said the nobleman, "see thee writing again." "I will do so," said Tanwyn, and he wrote, "Man's best candle is discretion." "Whither art thou going?" asked the nobleman. "Into the world to earn my livelihood," said Tanwyn. "Thou art the man I want," said the nobleman; "wilt thou come with me and be my steward, to manage my household and my property?" "I will," said Tanwyn, and he went to live with the nobleman.

He performed his duties with such wisdom and good will and justice that all who came to visit the nobleman praised the new steward greatly. In the course of time Tanwyn's fame for discretion and honourable dealing aroused his master's envy. The more men lauded Tanwyn, the more envious did the nobleman become, until he at last took counsel with his lady about putting him to death. She in her love for her lord bethought her of a way to compass Tanwyn's destruction. The nobleman had on his estate some lime-burners: the lady went to them and promised them a great sum of money if they would throw into the kiln the first man who should come to them with a vessel of mead. She told her lord of her stratagem, and the two, filling a large vessel with mead, ordered Tanwyn to take it to the lime-burners. Tanwyn took the vessel and carried it towards the kiln. On the way he heard in a house the voice of an old and godly man preaching the word of God, and according to his father's instruction turned into the house and listened for a considerable time to the preacher's words.

Meanwhile, the nobleman concluding that by that time Tanwyn must be reduced to ashes, proceeded to the kiln with another vessel of mead as a reward to the lime-burners. When he arrived there, he was seized by the lime-burners and thrown into the fire, where he perished miserably. Thus did envy burn itself.

The Bride from the Red Lake

A FARMER was one misty day fishing in Llyn Coch, the Red Lake, in the Forest of Snowdon. A sudden gust of wind cleared a road through the grey vapour that hung over the lake, and revealed a little man standing on a ladder and busily engaged in thatching a stack. The stack and ladder rested on the surface of the lake. In a few minutes the vision faded away, and there was nothing but rippling water to be seen in the place where the hay and thatcher had been observed.

After this the farmer often used to visit the lake, but he saw nothing remarkable until one hot day in autumn, when riding by the lake he took his horse into the water to drink.

While the animal was slaking its thirst he was looking idly at the ripples, when to his intense astonishment he became aware of a most lovely face just beneath the surface a little distance from him, looking up at him. As he gazed bewildered, the head and shoulders which belonged to the face emerged from the water. He leaped from his horse and rushed towards the damsel; when he got there the vision had vanished, but it instantly reappeared in another part of the lake. Again he rushed towards it, and again it disappeared. This happened a third time, and a fourth time, and a fifth, after which the farmer gave up the chase and went disconsolately home.

The next day the farmer went to the lake once more, and sat down by the margin in the hope of seeing the beautiful damsel again, but for a long time there was no sign of her. To beguile the tedium of waiting, he took out of his pocket some apples of rare and delicious quality which had been given to him by a neighbour, and began to munch one of them. Suddenly the lady appeared in all her dazzling beauty almost close to him, and begged him to throw her one of his apples. “If you want an apple you must fetch it yourself,” said the farmer, and he held out the tempting morsel, exhibiting its beautiful red and green sides. Upon this she came up quite close, and as she took the apple from his left hand, he seized tight hold of her with his right and held her fast. She screamed at the top of her voice, and an old man, with a long white beard and a wreath of water-lilies, appeared out of the midst of the lake. “Oh, mortal, what wouldest thou with my daughter?” he asked of the farmer. The farmer said that he would break his heart unless the nymph of the lake consented to be his wife. After much pleading the father agreed to the union on one condition, which was that the young man should not strike his wife with clay. The wedding took place at once, and the couple lived together in the greatest happiness.

One day the wife expressed a desire for some of those same delicious apples with which the farmer had tempted her out of the lake. Off went the husband to the neighbour who grew them, and brought back not only some apples, but a beautiful young sapling, bearing the same apple, as a present from their friend. This they at once proceeded to set, he digging and she holding the tree until the hole should be deep enough to plant it in. “It is deep enough now,” said the farmer, and for luck he threw out the last spadeful of clay over his shoulder. He did not look which way he threw it, and it fell right against the breast of his wife. She no sooner received the blow than she cried with a great and exceeding bitter cry. “Fare thee well, dear husband,” she said, and ran into the lake and disappeared beneath the smooth and glassy waters.

A Fairy Dog

GOING home from Pentre Voelas Church, the good wife of Hafod y Gareg found a little dog in an exhausted state on the ground. She took it up tenderly and carried it home in her apron. This she did partly from natural kindliness of heart and partly from fear, because she remembered what had happened to her cousin of Bryn Heilyn. She had come across a strange little dog and treated it cruelly. The fairies had come to her as she was taking *glasdwr* (which is butter-milk diluted with water) to the hayfield. They seized her and enquired whether she would travel above wind, mid wind or below wind. She ought to have selected the middle course, which would have meant a pleasant voyage through the air at a moderate height, equally removed from the clouds and the earth. Above wind is a giddy and terrible passage through the thin ether between the worlds, and it was well that she did not choose it. But the course she made choice of, below wind, was almost as bad, because she was snatched through miry bog and swampy lea, through brambles and briars, until all her clothes were torn off her body, and she was brought back to her home scratched and bleeding all over.

The good wife of Hafod y Gareg had no desire for any such excursions, and she made a nice soft bed for the fairy dog in the pantry, and fed it well. The following day a company of fairies came to the farmhouse to make enquiries about it. She told them it was safe and sound, and that they were welcome to take it away. In gratitude for her kindness, they asked her which she would prefer, a clean or a dirty cowyard. Reflecting that you cannot have a clean cowyard unless your cows are very few in number, she gave the right answer, a dirty cowyard. She found two cows for every one she had possessed before, and their milk made the best butter in the whole neighbourhood.

Grace's Well

AT THE south-east corner of Glasfryn lake, in the parish of Llangybi, is a well called Ffynnon Grassi, or Grace's Well. In the olden time it was a fairy well, and Grassi was in charge of it. Her duty was to keep the cover always on the well, except when water was being drawn. One evening she forgot to close the well, and the water gushed out. It flowed strongly and ceaselessly, but so noiseless was the flow that the fairies did not notice it. At last it overwhelmed one of their dancing rings, and they perceived and stopped the overflow, not, however, before Glasfryn lake had been formed.

When she saw the result of her negligence, Grassi, overcome with remorse, walked to and fro on the piece of ground which is now called Cae'r Ladi, "the Lady's Field," wringing her hands and weeping and moaning. The fairies seized her and changed her into a swan. In this form she haunted the lake which her forgetfulness had caused for six score years, after which time the fairies allowed her to resume her human shape. At any rate, there is to be seen about two hours after midnight, on certain nights in the year, a tall lady with lovely features and large bright eyes, dressed in white silk and a white velvet bonnet, wandering up and down the high ground of Cae'r Ladi, weeping and wailing. If she is not Grassi who is she?

The Fairy Password

WHEN a farm servant was once lying in hiding near the Ynys Geinon Rock, waiting for some perverse rabbits to enter his net, he saw a little man going up to that great mass of stone. On his uttering a curious little word, a door opened in the face of the rock: he went in, and the door closed behind him.

Dai (every other man in South Wales has this pretty name) thought he would see what would happen if he uttered the same little word as the little man had used. He tried the experiment: the door opened for him also, and he went into the rock. But he could not shut the stone door behind him, and when he saw that it weighed at least three or four tons, he did not want to do so. At this juncture a little man came running towards Dai shouting, "Shut the door, shut the door, the candles are guttering with the draught." With that he uttered another curious little word, and the door shut of its own accord. Then he noticed the intruder and called his companions. They made great sport of Dai, but as he was ruddy and of a fair complexion they treated him kindly.

He found that there were underground passages running in all directions: they could get to the Cave of Tan yr Ogof, near Craig y Nos Castle, the Caves of Ystrad Fellte, the Garn Goch, and other places by them. He learned, too, much about their habits: these fairies were dreadful thieves, always stealing milk and butter and cheese from farm-dairies.

After he had been with them for about two years they let him go, and gave him a hatful of guineas to take with him, for they had great stores of gold. He told his master all about his experiences when he returned, but it would have been better if he had kept his knowledge to himself. His master thought it was a great pity that so much gold should lie idle, and opening the stone door by means of the password which Dai had learned, he brought from the cave enough guineas, half-guineas and seven-and-sixpenny pieces to fill his salt chest. But he became too greedy; and when he went to the cave to fetch still more money, the fairies caught him, and he never returned. When Dai went to look for him, he found his four quarters hanging behind the stone door: he was so frightened that he never again ventured to use the password, nor would he reveal it to anyone, so that this very useful bit of information has perished, which is a very great pity.

St. Winifred's Well

IN THE seventh century there lived a virgin of the name of Winifred, the daughter of noble parents: her father, Thewith, was a powerful noble, and her mother was sister to St. Beuno. After founding his monastery at Clynnog, St. Beuno visited his relatives in Flintshire, and, obtaining from his brother-in-law a piece of land, caused a church and convent to be erected on it; in charge of the convent he placed his niece Winifred.

Caradoc, a neighbouring Prince, struck by her great beauty, tried to gain her in marriage, but, having dedicated herself to the service of God, Winifred would not listen to his suit. Thereupon the Prince attempted to carry her off by force, but she escaped from his hands and fled. Caradoc, enraged at his disappointment, pursued her, drew his sword and cut off her head. He instantly received the reward of his crime: he fell down dead, and the earth opening, swallowed his impious corpse. The severed head bounded down the hill and stopped near the church. Where it rested a great spring burst forth. St. Beuno, coming out of the church, where he had been preaching, took up the head and carried it to the corpse. After praying to God, he joined it to the body, and the virgin was restored to life, nor was there any sign of the wound to be seen other than a slender white line encircling her neck. Winifred lived fifteen years after this, and became the abbess of a convent at Gwytherin, in Denbighshire.

The spring which burst forth on the spot where her head

rested is still flowing, and its stones are annually spotted with blood in commemoration of the miracle. Ever since it has been believed to have virtues like those of the Pool of Bethesda, and great multitudes of sick folk, blind, halt and withered step into it to be made whole of their diseases.

The Ancients of the World

THERE was once an Eagle living in the woods of Gwernabwy: he and his mate had young ones till the ninth generation and far beyond that; then the old mother eagle died, leaving her husband a lonely widower, without anyone to console and cheer him in his old age. In the sadness of his heart he thought it would be well if he married an old widow of his own age. Hearing of the old Owl of Cwm Cawlyd, he took it into his head to make her his second wife, but before doing so, being anxious not to degrade his race, he determined to make enquiries about her.

He had an old friend, older than himself, the Stag of Rhedynfre, in Gwent. He went to him and asked the age of the old Owl. The Stag answered him thus: "Seest thou, my friend, this oak by which I lie? It is now but a withered stump, without leaves or branches, but I remember seeing it an acorn on the top of the chief tree of this forest. An oak is three hundred years in growing, and after that three hundred years in its strength and prime, and after that three hundred years in returning unto earth. Upwards of sixty years of the last hundred of this oak are passed, and the Owl has been old since I first remember her. Nor does anyone of my kindred know her age. But I have a friend who is much older than I, the Salmon of Llyn Llifon. Go to him and ask him if he knows aught of the age and history of the old Owl."

The Eagle went to the Salmon, who answered him thus: "I have a year over my head for every gem on my skin and for every egg in my roe, but the Owl was old when first I remember her. But I have a friend who is much older than I, the Ousel of Cilgwri. Haply he knows more about the Owl than I do."

The Eagle went and found the Ousel sitting on a hard flint, and asked him if he knew aught of the age and history of the Owl. The Ousel, answering, said: "Seest thou this flint on which I sit? I have seen it so large that it would have taken three hundred yoke of the largest oxen to move it, and it has never been worn away save by my cleaning my beak upon it once every night before going to sleep, and striking the tip of my wing against it after rising in the morning. Yet never have I known the Owl younger or older than she is to-day. But I have a friend who is much older than I, the Toad of Cors Fochno. Go to him and ask him if he knows aught of the age and history of the Owl."

The Eagle went to the Toad, who answered him thus: "I never eat any food save the dust of the earth, and I never eat half enough to satisfy me. Seest thou the great hills around this bog? I have seen the place where they stand level ground. I have eaten all the earth they contain, though I eat so little for fear lest the mould of the earth should be consumed before my death. Yet never have I known the Owl anything else but an old grey hag who cried to-whit-to-whoo in the woods in the long winter nights, and scared children with her voice even as she does to-day."

Then the Eagle saw he could marry her without bringing disgrace or degradation on his tribe. And so it was from the courtship of the Eagle that it was known which were the oldest creatures in the world. They are the Eagle of Gwernabwy, the Stag of Rhedynfre, the Salmon of Llyn Llifon, the Ousel of Cilgwri, the Toad of Cors Fochno, and the Owl of Cwm Cawlyd, and the oldest of them all is the Owl.

Nansi Llwyd and the Dog of Darkness

NANSI LLWYD was walking in the dusk of the evening towards Aberystruth, and she was in a very bad temper, for she was longing to get married, and according to all the omens she never would.

The previous night being All Hallow Eve, she and Gweno Dafydd and Sian Probert had been seeking to learn the future. Sian and Gweno were satisfied with the results of the *rhamanta* or divination, but Nansi was cruelly disappointed. What made it worse was that they had all made a great preparation for the test. Nansi had slept not long before on an oat-straw bed, Gweno had spent a night on a mattress made of the leaves of the mountain ash mixed with the seeds of spring fern, and Sian had a pillow of maiden hair on which she had laid her comely head. Nor had they confined themselves to one test. First of all they experimented with yarn. Taking a ball of yarn, Nansi and Gweno doubled the threads and tied tiny pieces of wood along them so as to form a little ladder. Then they went upstairs together, and, opening the window, threw the ladder to the ground. Nansi began winding the yarn back, saying the while:

> "I am winding,
> Who is holding?"

This she did three times, and no lover made his appearance, so that her chance of marriage for one year was lost. When

Gweno performed the ceremony, on the other hand, Cadwaladr Rhys, a most desirable young man, appeared.

The water-in-basin test was still more unsatisfactory. Three basins were placed on the table, one filled with clear spring water, one with muddy water, and the other empty. The three girls were led blindfolded to the table, and told to place their hands on the basins. Gweno put her hand on the basin containing clear spring water, which showed that she was to marry a bachelor. Sian touched the basin with the muddy water, which meant she was to wed a widower. Nansi's hand lighted on the empty basin. This meant that a single life was in store for her. Now, to remain unmarried for one year is not very serious, but lifelong maidenhood was a prospect which made Nansi feel first hot and then cold.

She consoled herself with the reflection that the water-in-basin test was not absolutely certain, and she decided to try the pullet's egg test. She took the first egg of a pullet, cut it through the middle, filled one half-shell with wheaten flour, added salt to the other, and then made a cake out of the egg, the flour and the salt. One-half of this cake she ate: the other half she placed in the foot of her left stocking under her pillow as she went to bed. Then she said her prayers, and lay down to sleep. Now she ought to have dreamt of some man coming to her bedside to offer her a drink of water: this man would be her future husband. But troubled as her dreams were, no human being figured in them, and she felt when she got up that all the sunshine had gone out of life. She became still more sad when she went to examine the movements of the snail she had placed under a basin early the day before. If it had been a right-minded snail it would have moved about and traced the initials of her future husband's name. But the slimy sluggard had remained motionless, and Nansi hurled it viciously out of the window. If it did not sustain serious injuries from the fall, it was not Nansi's fault. All this evidence that she was to be an old maid made Nansi very bad tempered, and she had not recovered when she took her walk.

Suddenly a horse came galloping down the road, and she was all but knocked down by the furious animal. She recognised the horse as that of Jenkin Pari, whom she had noticed going to market that morning, and she wondered how it had come to pass that the steed was bolting home at such a pace without its rider. As she proceeded on her way, thinking about the horse, she saw two large shining eyes, which drew nearer and nearer. Presently the body and limbs of a large spotted dog loomed into sight. Nansi had a mastiff with her, and she tried to set it on the strange hound. In vain: the mastiff crouched frightened at her feet and whined piteously. The great dog with the fiery eyes came right up to her, and Nansi, to protect herself, kicked at it as hard as she could with her right foot. Her foot was paralysed, and when a circle of fire surrounded the hound she had kicked, and it squatted on its haunches, setting up a loud, horrible unearthly howl, she fell senseless on the ground.

She was discovered, still unconscious, by old Antoni, Jenkin Pari's farm bailiff. He, seeing his master's horse standing trembling by the stable door, had set out in search of the farmer. He came across Nansi, and brought her to by dashing cold water on her face. Going further along the road he found Jenkin Pari lying in a dead faint on his back in the mud. Jenkin said when he came to himself that the horse had shied, reared and tumbled him off. Jenkin was none the worse for his fall, but Nansi's right leg was as black as coal until the day of her death. Had she not been in so bad a temper, she would have realised that it was Gwyllgi, or Dog of Darkness, that had come along the road, and she would no more have touched it than she would have refused an offer of marriage.

An Adventure in the Big Bog

A YOUNG harper of Bala was asked to play at a wedding in a farmhouse near Yspytty Ifan. When the joyous company broke up late at night he set off for home like the rest, but he had a much longer way to go than anyone else. When he was crossing the mountain a dense fog came on, and he lost his way. He was wandering about trying to find the path again, when he suddenly stepped into the Gors Fawr, "the big bog." The treacherous crust swayed for an instant under his tread, and then it broke. The soft mud oozed round his ankles, and he felt himself going further and further down. He tried to raise himself on his harp, but the only result of this was to plunge the beloved instrument into the bog, and he himself sank lower and lower. At last, with a desperate effort, he hurled himself full length upon the surface. The yielding crust caved under his body, and he clutched at the surface grass, but he only plucked the tufts from their roots. They gave him no hold. With every fresh effort to save himself he sank deeper. The gurgling slime sucked him down, down, down, and in the anguish of his soul he threw his head back in one last wild scream.

His cry was just dying away when the fog suddenly cleared, and a little man appeared on the brink of the bog. He threw a rope to the harper, who, after a great struggle, fastened it round his body under the arms. The little man pulled and pulled and gradually drew the harper out of the mire. He took him to a house blazing with light hard by, where there was singing and dancing and much revelry. The harper was given fine clean clothes, and after drinking a flagon of delicious mead he recovered sufficiently from the fright which the fall into the bog had given him to join in the festivity which was going on. There was a little lady there whom the company addressed as Olwen. She was the most beautiful little lady that the harper had ever seen and the best dancer. With her he danced hour after hour, and the only bitter in his cup of sweet was the thought that his beloved harp was in the slimy blackness of the Gors. When the whole company retired to rest he was put in a bed as soft as the softest down, and he thought he had reached a very heaven of delight.

But next morning he was awakened, not by a kiss from Olwen, but by the Plas Drain shepherd's dog licking his lips: he found himself lying by the wall of a sheepfold, and there was no trace of the house in which he had spent such a happy night. His clothes were all caked with bog mud, and his harp, which was in a clump of rushes at his feet, was black with the same defilement.

The Pwca of the Trwyn

A PRANKSOME goblin once took up his abode at the Trwyn Farm, in the parish of Mynyddislwyn, and became known throughout the country as Pwca'r Trwyn, or the Pwca of the Trwyn. How he got there is not known. One story says that he once lived at Pant y gaseg. Moses, one of the farm servants of the Trwyn, came to Pant y gaseg for a jug of barm, and the Pwca was heard to say, "The Pwca is going away now in this jug of barm, and he'll never come back," and he never was heard of at Pant y gaseg again. Another story tells that a servant of Pant y gaseg let fall a ball of yarn, and the Pwca said, "I am going in this ball, and I'll go to the Trwyn and never come back." Directly after this the ball was seen to roll down the hill-side and across the valley, ascending the hill on the other side and trundling along briskly across the mountain top of this new abode.

Anyhow, the Pwca came to the Trwyn, and though he remained invisible he became very friendly with Moses. He did all his work for him with great ease. For instance, he threshed a whole barnful of corn in a single night. Once, indeed, he gave him a good beating for doubting his word, but apart from that the two remained on the best possible terms for a long time. Moses went away, however, with David Morgan, the Jacobite, to join the Young Pretender, and never came back again.

After this the Pwca transferred his affections to Blodwen, one of the servant-girls, and very useful he proved to her. He did everything for her, washing, ironing, spinning and twisting wool—at the spinning wheel he was remarkably handy. No one was allowed to catch a sight of him, but he became very talkative, and often used to speak from out of an oven by the side of the hearth. He told Blodwen that it was very mean of her not to provide him with food and drink for helping her so much, and after this she used, with her master Job John Harri's permission, to place a bowl of fresh milk and a slice of white bread (the latter was a great luxury at that time) on the hearth every night for him before going to bed. By the morning the bread was eaten and the bowl empty. This fare made the Pwca light-hearted, and he used to make music o' nights with Job John Harri's fiddle, and very merry rollicking music it was.

One evening he revealed part of himself. The servant-girls were comparing their hands as to size and whiteness, when a voice from the ceiling was heard to say, "The Pwca's hand is the fairest and smallest." "Show it, then," said Blodwen, who used to speak quite freely to him. Immediately a hand appeared from the ceiling, small, fair, and beautifully formed, with a large gold ring on the little finger.

It was Blodwen's fault that the Pwca became troublesome. One night, in a spirit of mischief, she drank the milk and ate the bread that were usually provided for him, leaving him some stale crusts of barley bread and a bowlful of dirty water. It would have been better for her not to have done it. When she got up next morning he suddenly sprang from some corner, and, seizing her by the neck, began to beat her and kick her from one end of the house to the other, until she screamed for mercy.

After this the Pwca became freakish, and played all sorts of pranks. He began his games by knocking at the door, but when it was opened there was no one to be seen. Then he did all sorts of mischief about the house, and in the cowhouses and stable. He harassed the oxen when they ploughed and drew them after him everywhere, plough and all, nor could anyone prevent them.

The neighbours came to hear about these goings on, and one of them, Thomas Evans by name, said he would take a gun and shoot the Pwca. As Job John Harri was coming home one night from a journey the Pwca met him in the lane and said, "There is a man come to your house to shoot me, but you shall see how I will beat him." So Job went on to the house and found Thomas Evans there with his gun, breathing all manner of dire threats against the wicked sprite. Suddenly stones flew from all directions at Thomas and hurt him badly. The members of the household of the Trwyn got round him, thinking to protect him, but the stones still struck him. The curious part of the whole thing was that they never touched anyone else. At last Thomas Evans took his gun and ran home as fast as his legs could carry him, and never again did he talk of shooting the Pwca.

Job John Harri went to a fair, and night overtook him on the mountain as he was returning home. Somehow or other, though the path was quite familiar to him, he lost his way. Whether it was owing to the darkness or from some other cause (there are influences at fairs which cause many to stray from the right path) is uncertain; at any rate he wandered onwards in different directions over the mountain in much doubt and perplexity. At last he was brought to a full stop against a stone wall. As he was rubbing his forehead, which had got the worst of the collision with the wall, and considering the situation, a light suddenly arose upon the waste at a short distance to his right. "There is some one with a lantern," he said to himself, and he determined to follow in his wake. As he walked on he noticed that there were two very remarkable things about the light. One was that however fast or however slow he walked, the light kept at just the same distance from him. Again, it kept so near the ground that the arm which bore it must have belonged to a person of exceptionally short stature. Job concluded that it was a child carrying a lantern. He followed the light for several miles, when it suddenly stopped. Job had by this time come well nigh up to it, and was about to hail its bearer when the sound of a foaming torrent arose to his ears. Just then the bearer of the light took a flying leap and landed some thirty yards away. The light blazed forth brilliantly, and Job found himself on the brink of a frightful precipice. On the other side of the yawning chasm was a tiny little man, as naked as a new-born babe, with long hair and pointed ears, and a maliciously ugly expression on his face, peering down into the gorge (it was afterwards called Cwm Pwca).

When he saw that Job had not fallen into the trap towards which he had led him, he uttered a loud shrill laugh and douted the light. Job was afraid to move, and remained on the spot, stiff with terror, until daylight appeared, when he made his way home. After that the Pwca was never heard or seen at the Trywn.

John Gethin and the Candle

THERE once lived at Ystradgynlais a wizard with an iron hand. By means of his magic he discovered that there was a great treasure hidden in Mynydd y Drum, and that he could secure it if he could only get some plucky fellow to spend a night with him on the mountain near the rock under which the gold and silver lay.

For a long time he could not secure a companion. He approached all his friends and acquaintances in vain: they were afraid and refused to have anything to do with such a perilous adventure. At last, however, John Gethin, who was a reckless youth and said that he cared for nothing in heaven above, or in the earth beneath or in the water under the earth, said he would accompany the man with the iron hand on condition that he received half the treasure.

One dark night the twain went to the mountain and took up their stand on a greensward near the rock under which the wizard said the treasure was concealed. "Now," said the magician, "I am going to call upon the spirit which guards the treasure to present himself before us." He put on a robe of black covered with talismanic characters, girded himself with snake-skins tied together, and placed on his head a cap of sheepskin with a high crown bearing a plume of pigeons' feathers. In his hand he had a whip, the thong of which was made of the skin of an eel and the handle of bone. With this he traced two circles on the sward touching each other like the figure 8. After that he took a great black book and lit a candle and stepped into one of the circles.

"Stand in the middle of the other circle," said he to Gethin, "and whatever happens, do not step out of the ring." Gethin did as he was told.

The wizard opened his book and read: "I adjure and invocate thee by the silence of the night and by the holy rites of magic and by the number of the infernal legions, that without delay thou present thyself here and answer my demand by the force of the words contained in this book." This he repeated thrice.

First there appeared a monstrous bull, bellowing dreadfully, but the plucky Gethin held his ground, and the bull vanished. Then a gigantic goat came and rushed full pelt at Gethin, but as he did not move the goat also melted into thin air. Next a huge bristly boar charged at him, and an immense fire-breathing lion crouched and leapt at him, but Gethin stood motionless, and as soon as these fearful apparitions crossed the circle drawn by the magician they vanished into space. Then a great fly-wheel of fire, blazing brightly and roaring loudly, made straight for poor Gethin. For a moment he lost heart and swerved out of the ring. No sooner had he done this than the fly-wheel of fire assumed the shape of the Enemy of Mankind, and began to haul Gethin away. The man with the iron hand seized hold of him and tried to get him back. Poor Gethin nearly parted in half in the struggle between the two.

The Enemy of Mankind was getting the better of the tug of war, when the wizard said, "By the power of the East, Athanaton, of the West, Orgon, of the South, Boralim, of the North, Glauron, I charge and command thee to suffer this man to live while this candle lasts." The Evil One let go his hold of Gethin and vanished. Thereupon the wizard immediately blew out the candle and gave it to Gethin. "Had you not swerved out of the circle," he said, "all would have been well, but as you disobeyed my command, this is the utmost respite that I can secure for you. Put the candle away in a cool place. As long as the candle lasts your life will be safe."

Gethin went home and preserved the piece of candle very carefully, stowing it away in the coldest place he could find. But as time went on he found it was wasting away, although it was never lighted. Gethin was never the same after his fearful night on the mountain, and when he found the candle wasting away he took to his bed. As the candle wasted away he did the same, and after some years both came to an end at the same time. The wizard attended him during his last hours, and those who carried the coffin, which was supposed to contain Gethin's mortal remains, found it very light. The story went that Gethin's body disappeared out of the coffin before it was nailed up, and that the wizard put a lump of clay there instead to save appearances, but no one was bold enough to open the coffin to find out the truth.

Fetching a Halter

A VERY large company came together to hold a merry evening at Bwlch Mwrchan, a farmhouse close by Lake Gwynan, in Snowdonia. It was a stormy night. The wind whistled and howled in the woods, tearing the trees like matchsticks. The night was dark and shreds of heavy clouds floated over the narrow valley, dimly visible and seeming like terrible and ghastly spectres. Lake Gwynan boiled like a boisterous sea, and the spray of its waves was dashed by the wind against the walls and windows of the house.

The weather affected the spirits of the company and gave a melancholy tone to the songs and stories. Disappointed at the turn things had taken, the good man of the house thought he would create a diversion and said, "I will wager that not one of you young men is brave enough to go to the Hafotty, in Cwm Merch, and fetch the halter which I left there."

Now, the Hafotty was about a mile from the house, and the pathway to it was narrow, rugged, steep, and in every way bad. Not one of the company liked the idea of turning out on such a night, not only on account of the weather, but because of the unearthly terrors which might be encountered. The Gwrach y Rhibyn might well be out on such a night. This hideous hag has red hair as coarse as a horse's tail, falling down in rough ringlets over her bony shoulders. Her two cheek-bones project like two ridges, and her curved nose almost meets her pointed chin. Her eyes flash fire from their deep sockets, and she appears in front of the pedestrian with long bony arms uplifted, shouting in a cold, shrill voice, "Woe is me, woe is me." Then is the heart of the bravest melted and his knees smite one against another. The Cwn Annwn, too, the Hounds of Hell, might be heard howling in such a tempest. They are blood-red in colour, and they drip with gore, and their eyes and teeth are of fire. The devil is their huntsman, and they give chase in the air. Their quarry is the souls of evil livers which they hunt to their allotted place of torment. Their cry makes the blood of the hearer freeze in his veins.

It was no wonder, therefore, that the youths present hesitated to accept the challenge of their host. The women-folk, then, began to taunt them with their cowardice. At last, stung by their reproaches, a man from Nant Gwynan said he would sally forth. Against the Hounds of Hell he protected himself by taking with him a cross, for when this is shown to them they fly in the greatest terror. But he saw no one worse than himself, and heard nothing more unearthly than the roar of the wind as he fought his way up. In spite of the storm, the darkness, and the steep winding path, he managed to reach Cwm Merch in safety. When within a short distance of the Hafotty he saw a light within, which was strange, as no one lived there except in the summer, and the place was too outlandish for any stranger to have strayed thither from his way. He went on, not without misgivings, and as he drew near he heard the doleful sound of painful moans. He paused and listened, thinking it might be the wind. But as he went on the moaning became more distinct: a woman was groaning in dreadful pain. He hastened to the door, but found it secured from within. He peered in through some of the cracks, and the sight he saw made gooseflesh come all over him. There was a little woman bound hand and foot, and two men were placing her before a blazing fire to be roasted alive. Stepping back he flung himself upon the door with his whole strength, and sent it spinning into the middle of the Hafotty. Swift as thought he cut the woman loose from the bonds that held her. He then looked round for the two men whom he had seen torturing her, but both had disappeared. When the woman had sufficiently recovered he led her down to Bwlch Mwrchan, where he introduced her to the assembled company with the words, "This is the halter I found in the Hafotty."

At daybreak all went in search of the two monsters. They found their bodies at the foot of a steep cliff, stone cold. The little woman soon recovered from her injuries and married her deliverer. Most of the inhabitants of Nant Gwynan to-day are their descendants.

Dai Sion's Homecoming

Dai Sion, the shoemaker's son, living near Pencader, in Carmarthenshire, chanced upon a fairy circle on the mountain and felt an irresistible inclination to dance. He just gave a turn, as he thought, to air his legs, and immediately jumped out of the ring again and proceeded to return home.

He had not gone far when he paused in amazement. Where was he? All was changed. Instead of an uncultivated waste, tilled land met his eye. There were houses where grouse had risen scared by his footfall. Where his father's circular wattled mud hut had been, there now stood a fine stone house. "Ah," said Dai to himself, "this is some fairy trick to deceive my eyes; it is not ten minutes since I stepped into the circle, and no one could have built my father a real house in that time." Thinking then that he was under some spell, he regarded all that he beheld as imaginary and unsubstantial, and hastened towards his father's dwelling. A thorn hedge stood right across the path which he had known from a child. He rubbed his eyes and felt the hedge with his hand to test its reality. A thorn ran into his finger and convinced him that the barrier was solid. "This is no fairy hedge, anyhow," he said, "nor judging by the age of the thorns was it grown in a few minutes' time." So he climbed over it and walked on. He reached the farmyard, and all seemed so strange that he felt himself an intruder. "Tango, Tango," said Dai, "though you have grown and changed your colour, don't you know me?" But the brute only barked the more. "Surely," he said to himself, "I have lost my way and am wandering through some unknown parish; but no, yonder is the Gareg Hir," and he stood staring at the Long Stone which still stands on the mountain south of Pencader and commemorates some battle long ago. As he gazed he heard footsteps behind him, and turning, beheld the occupant of the stone house, who had come out to see why his dog was barking. Dai's clothes were so ragged and he looked so wan that the farmer's Welsh heart went out to him. "Who are you, poor man?" he asked. "I know who I was," answered Dai, "but I do not know who I am now. I was the son of a shoemaker who lived in this place this morning." "My poor fellow," said the farmer, "you have lost your senses. This house was built by my great-grandfather and repaired by my father, and none but members of my family have ever lived here. What was your father's name?"

"Sion Ifan y Crydd," was the answer. "I never heard of such a man," said the farmer, shaking his head. "Well, I do not know what to make of it," said Dai; "anyhow, I know the Long Stone well enough. It is but an hour since I was robbing a hawk's nest close by it." "But where have you been since?" asked the farmer. "I stepped into a fairy ring on the mountain, had a turn round and stepped out again." "Ah, you have been with the fairies?" said the farmer. "Old Catti Sion at Pencader is the one who knows most about the fairies about here. We will go down to see her, she will probably be able to tell us something. But come into the house to have some food before we go." With this he beckoned Dai to follow him, and led the way; but hearing behind him the sound of footsteps growing fainter and fainter, he turned round, and to his horror saw Dai ap Sion crumbling in an instant into a thimbleful of black ashes.

The farmer later on paid a visit to old Catti. He went to the wretched hovel in which she lived and knocked at the door. Getting no answer he entered and called out, "Catti Sion, Catti Sion, where are you?" A thin quavering voice said, "I am in my bed." The Farmer turned and saw a barricade of thick gorse, so closely packed and piled up that no bed was to be seen. "What is all this gorse for, Catti?" asked the farmer. "It is because of the Fair Family," said Catti; "they will never leave me alone. If I am up, they will sit upon the table making faces at me: they turn my milk sour and spill my tea, and before I put up this gorse they would not leave me at peace in my bed. But they cannot get through this, it pricks them so bad, and then I get some rest." "It is a splendid device, Catti," said the farmer, "but, tell me, do you remember a man called Sion Ifan y Crydd—was there such a man?" "Well," said Catti, "I have some faint recollection of hearing my grandfather relate that Sion's son was lost one morning, and they never heard of him afterwards, so that it was said he was taken by the fairies. Sion's cottage stood somewhere near your house."

Melangell's Lambs

BROCHWEL, the Prince of Powys, upon a certain day in the year of our Lord 604, was hunting in a place called Pennant. His hounds started a hare, and pursued it into a dense thicket. Following them into the thicket, he saw a beautiful maiden on her knees praying devoutly to God. The hare was lying on the folds of her garment, facing the hounds boldly. The Prince shouted, "Catch her, catch her!" but the more he urged his hounds on, the further did they retreat, and at last they fled away, howling with terror. The Prince, astonished at the strange behaviour of his hounds, turned to the maiden and asked her who she was. "I am the daughter of a King of Ireland," she answered, "and because my father desired to wed me to one of his chiefs, I fled from my native soil, and, God guiding me, came to this desert place, where for fifteen years I have served God without seeing the face of any man." The Prince enquired her name, and she replied that she was called Melangell (the Latin form of the name is Monacella). Thereupon the Prince broke forth in these words, "O most worthy Melangell, I perceive that thou art the handmaiden of the true God. Because it hath pleased Him for thy merits to give protection to this little wild hare from the attack and pursuit of the ravening hounds, I give and present to thee with willing mind these my lands for the service of God, to be a perpetual asylum and refuge. If any men or women flee hither to seek thy protection, provided they do not pollute thy sanctuary, let no prince or chieftain be so rash towards God as to attempt to drag them forth."

Melangell passed the rest of her days in this lonely place, sleeping on bare rock. Many were the miracles which she wrought for those who sought refuge in her sanctuary with pure hearts. The little wild hares were ever under her special protection, and that is why they are called "Melangell's lambs." Even now, if a hare is pursued by hounds and someone shouts after it, "God and Melangell be with thee," it will escape.

Syfaddon Lake

SYFADDON LAKE was once a beautiful estate belonging to a great lady. A young warrior from Brecon, of gentle birth but no fortune, loved her, but she would not marry him because he was poor. He, prizing her more than the welfare of his soul, met a rich merchant in a lonely spot and murdered him. Then, showing his lady love the gold and gems which he had taken from the body of his victim, he again asked her to be his wife. This time she consented. She was, however, curious to know how he had procured his wealth, though she did not care whether honestly or otherwise, and he told her. "Have you buried the corpse?" she asked. "No," said he. "You must go this night," she said, "and inter it: otherwise his kindred will find out that you have slain him, and they will avenge his blood."

The young warrior returned to the place where he had committed the foul deed and began to dig a grave. While he was delving he heard a loud voice proclaiming "Vengeance will come." Three times the warning was sounded, the second time more loudly than the first, and the third time in a voice like thunder. He threw down his spade in terror, and, flying to his lady love, told her what he had heard. "You must go back," she said, "and if you hear the voice again, ask when the punishment will fall." He obeyed, and this time he was allowed to bury the body in peace, but as he was turning homewards the dread voice again cried aloud, "Vengeance will come." The murderer plucked up courage to ask when. "In the lifetime of thy grandsons, great-grandsons, ascensors, and their children," was the answer. When he told his lady, "There is no reason for us to fear," said she; "we shall be under the mould long before."

The murderer and the lady felt safe enough, and their marriage was celebrated. They had sons and daughters who in their turn married and had children. These children multiplied, and the family became very numerous, until at last a descendant of the sixth direct generation was born. By this time the original pair were very old; but exulting in their prosperity (for they had flourished like the green bay-tree), they said one to the other, "We are great, rich and powerful, and our family is very numerous. We have lived according to our heart's delight, and have tasted of all the pleasures that life can give. Let us, before we die, make a great and splendid feast to all our family, and make merry with them before we bid them farewell."

A great and splendid feast was made, but when all the generations of the family were banqueting together, and the gaiety and mirth were at their height, the ground that was under them clave asunder and the earth opened and swallowed them up. Not one soul of them escaped, and a deluge of water overspread the place.

The Power of St. Tegla's Well

AT THE farm of Amnodd Bwll, at the foot of the Little Arenig, there once lived a farmer called Robert Wiliam, his wife Mari Tomos (in those days a woman did not lose her maiden name when she got married; that is only a recent fashion in Wales), and their only child, a boy who was known as Wiliam Robert (a son took his father's surname then as his Christian name). Now Wiliam was subject to fits, and in the summer when he attained the age of twelve his father and mother became terribly anxious about him, because so many signs of death followed one after another. One of the apple trees in the garden burst into blossom long before its time, which is very unlucky. The old cock which had for years behaved as well as any chanticleer in the county took to crowing in the middle of the night, and had to have his head chopped off before he would give up the fatal habit. Maria Tomos dreamed that she was at a wedding, which of course meant that she would before long attend a funeral. One night a bird flapped its wings against the window of the room in which Robert Wiliam and Mari Tomos slept, and the hearts of the worthy couple sank at the thought that it might have been the Corpse Bird, that weird, featherless bird, with wings of some leathery substance like those of a bat, which occasionally comes from the land of Illusion and Phantasy to beat its wings against the windows of houses which the King of Terrors is about to visit. Another night Robert Wiliam was so frightened that it was hours after his usual time when he crawled home, shaking like an aspen leaf. He was walking home by himself from a fair at Bala, by the side of the river Tryweryn, when he saw in the fading light a repulsive hag, clad in a long black gown trailing on the ground. Her face was deathly pale, with high cheek bones and deep-sunk lack-lustre eyes; she had great black projecting teeth, and a short nose with widely-distended nostrils. Her hair was grey and tangled. Her arms were skinny and shrivelled and of great length, out of all proportion to her body. She splashed in the water of the river with her hands, and made a most doleful noise. Robert Wiliam at first could not make out any words, but presently he distinctly heard, "My child, my child, my dear son," after uttering which words the hideous apparition vanished. The thought that he had seen the dreaded Cyhiraeth, and that her cry foreboded the death of his beloved boy, froze the blood in his veins, and the darkness had closed in before he could proceed on his homeward journey.

He had not gone much further when he saw a corpse candle moving before him along the road. It burned with a red flame, from which it was clear that it was not a woman who was doomed (a woman's candle is white), and the candle was small, indicating that a child was to die, for the size of corpse candles varies with the age of those whose death they foretell. This succession of nightly horrors almost paralysed Robert Wiliam, and he reached home more dead than alive.

The next day he went to consult a wise man who lived in Trawsfynydd, to see if there was any hope for his son. The wise man told him that his only chance was to take the boy to St. Tegla's Well, in Denbighshire, and instructed him what to do. Robert Wiliam took his son to Llandegla, and the following ceremony was performed. The boy went to the well after sunset, carrying a cock in a basket. First of all he walked round the well thrice, reciting the Lord's Prayer. Then he walked thrice round the church, again repeating the Paternoster. After this he entered the church, crept under the altar, and slept there until break of day, making the Bible his pillow and the communion cloth his coverlet. In the morning he placed sixpence on the altar, and leaving the cock in the church departed home with his father. Great was then the anxiety of Robert Wiliam to know the fate of the bird, for if it did not die in the church there would be no hope of cure. In about a week a messenger came to say that the bird had died, and that consequently the disease which had been transferred to it had died also. Whether this was so or not, it is curious that in spite of the apple tree which bloomed before its time, night-crowing cock, Corpse Bird, Cyhiraeth, and corpse candle, Wiliam Robert completely recovered from his illness and lived to a ripe old age.

The Men of Ardudwy

THE MEN of Ardudwy once upon a time found there were no maidens in their district for them to marry. In the Vale of Clwyd, on the other hand, there were so many maidens that husbands could not be found for all. There was a bitter feud, however, between the two districts, and the men of Ardudwy could not go a-wooing to the Vale in peace.

Those of the men of Ardudwy who wished to marry determined at last to steal wives for themselves, as they could not get them any other way, and taking advantage of the absence of the warriors of the Vale on an expedition they swooped down, and, snatching away the flower of the maidens, proceeded to carry them off to the mountains.

Messengers recalled the warriors of the Vale from their expedition, and a strong band of them started hot-foot in pursuit of the robbers. They overtook the fugitives near a lake among the mountains of Ffestiniog and summoned them to yield. The men of Ardudwy, though greatly outnumbered, scorned to surrender, and a fierce battle followed. All day long the noise of splintering spears, swords clashing on swords, and battleaxes crashing upon armour, rolled among the eternal mountains.

At first the men of the Vale rushed carelessly upon the men of Ardudwy, thinking that it was but a light task to overpower the little band, but so many of them fell that they drew off to order their attack better. They carefully marshalled the bravest of their number and charged; a desperate hand-to-hand struggle followed, but the men of Ardudwy, though they lost many good men, at last beat off the assault. They now feigned flight, but as the men of the Vale came on with wild cries and uproar, they wheeled round and cut down so many of them that they fled in disorder. They soon rallied, however, and delivered charge after charge. Time after time the men of Ardudwy flung them back, but they became fewer and fewer with each charge.

In the late afternoon there was a lull in the fray. Then the men of the Vale, gathering all their available force, delivered a last overwhelming charge on the weakened band. The men of Ardudwy sold their lives dearly, piling corpse upon corpse, but they were exhausted with wounds, their spears were shattered, and their swords were hacked and blunted. When the men of the Vale fell back to recover breath and strength, they found that there were only four of the defenders left alive. Though the number was so small, they did not close with them, but surrounded them and plied them with javelins and stones. Still the four of Ardudwy fought on while breath remained in their bodies; then one by one they sank down upon the pitiless storm of javelins, and at last there was nothing left of the gallant band but a heap of dead.

Even then, Death had not taken his full toll of victims. The maidens of the Vale had, ere their kindred came up, learned to love their captors. They had been stationed by them on the top of a precipice rising sheer and steep out of the lake, behind the position which was to be defended, and from here they had watched the long-drawn-out struggle. When the last of the men of Ardudwy fell, and the desperate fight was done, they plunged into the waters red with the blood of their lovers and kindred, like some great flight of white birds sweeping down from a wave-washed cliff down to the sea. The still waters leapt in foam: one loud shriek woke the air, and then silence reigned over all.

The lake was called after them Llyn y Morwynion, the Maidens' Lake, and not far from its margin great stones may still be seen marking the place where those who died in this great fight were buried.

The Parti-coloured Cow

A PARTI-COLOURED cow once appeared on the high moorlands of Denbighshire. Everyone who was in want of milk went to her, and however big a vessel was taken, it was always filled with rich milk. However often she was milked, it made no difference. This continued for a long time, and glad indeed were the people to avail themselves of her unfailing supply. At last a wicked witch determined to milk her dry. The hag took a riddle and milked and milked the parti-coloured cow until at last the milk ran dry. Immediately the cow went off to a lake near Cerrig y Drudion, bellowing horribly, and disappeared under its waters.

Striking a Corpse Candle

A CLERGYMAN in Carmarthenshire had a son who came home one night very late and found the doors locked against him. Not wishing to disturb his father and mother, and fearing also their reproaches and chidings, he went to the man-servant's bedroom, which was over the stable. He could not awake the man-servant, but while standing over him he saw a small light issue from his nostrils. He followed it out. It went over a foot-bridge which crossed a brook and on to the road which led up to the parish church. After following the corpse candle for some time, the young man, just to see what would happen, struck at it with his stick. It burst into sparks, but afterwards reunited into a flame as before, which stalked on until it finally disappeared in the churchyard.

Not long afterwards the man-servant died: at his funeral the bier broke at the spot where his master's son had struck at the corpse candle, and the coffin fell to the ground.

Hu Gadarn

THE RACE of the Cymry have not always dwelt in the Isle of Britain. In the dim past they inhabited the Summer Country called Deffrobani. While they sojourned there a great benefactor arose among them, to whom the name of Hu Gadarn, Hu the Mighty, was given. He invented the plough, and taught them to cultivate the ground. He divided them into communities, and gave them laws, whereby fighting and contention were lessened. Under his guidance they left the Summer Country, and crossing the Mor Tawch in coracles came to the Isle of Britain, and took possession of it under the protection of God and His peace. Before that time no one lived therein, but it was full of bears, wolves, beavers, and bannog oxen; no one, therefore, has a right to the Isle of Britain but the Cymry, for they first settled in it. They gave to it the name of the Honey Island, on account of the great quantity of honey they found (Britain is a later name). Hu ruled them with justice, establishing wise regulations and religious rites, and those who through God's grace had received poetic genius were made teachers of wisdom. Through their songs, history and truth were preserved throughout the ages until the act of writing was discovered.

Some time after they came to the Honey Island, the Cymry were much troubled by a monster called an afanc, which broke the banks of Llyn Llion, in which it dwelt, and flooded their lands. No spear, dart, or arrow made any impression upon its hide, so Hu Gadarn resolved to drag it from its abode and to place it where it could do no harm. A girl enticed it from its watery haunt, and while it slept with its head on her knees it was bound with long iron chains. When it woke and perceived what had been done, it got up, and, tearing off its sweetheart's breast in revenge, hurried to its old refuge. But the chains were fastened to Hu Gadarn's team of bannog oxen, which pulled it out of the lake and dragged it through the mountains to Llyn y Ffynnon Las, the Lake of the Green Well, in Cwm Dyli, in Snowdonia. A pass through which they laboured has ever since been called Bwlch Rhiw'r Ychen, the Pass of the Slope of the Oxen. One of the oxen dropped one of its eyes through its exertions in this defile, and the place is styled Gwaun Lygad Ych, the Moor of the Ox's Eye. A pool was formed where the eye fell, which is known as Pwll Llygad Ych, the Pool of the Ox's Eye; this pool is never dry, though no water rises in it or flows into it except when the rain falls, and no water flows out of it, but it is always of the same depth, reaching just to the knee-joint.

The afanc could not burst the banks of the Lake of the Green Well, but it is still dangerous to go near it. If a sheep falls into the lake it is at once dragged down to the bottom, and it is not safe even for a bird to fly across it.

The Devil's Bridge

ONE day in the olden time old Megan of Llandunach stood by the side of the river Mynach feeling very sorry for herself.

The Mynach was in flood, and roared down the wooded dingle in five successive falls, tumbling over three hundred feet in less than no time. Just below the place where Megan was standing, there was a great cauldron in which the water whirled, boiled and hissed as if troubled by some evil spirit: from the cauldron the river rushed and swirled down a narrow, deep ravine, and if the old woman had had an eye for the beauties of nature, the sight of the seething pot and the long shadowy cleft would have made her feel joyous rather than sorrowful.

But Megan at this time cared for none of these things, because her one and only cow was on the wrong side of the ravine, and her thoughts were centred on the horned beast which was cropping the green grass carelessly just as if it made no difference what side of the river it was on. How the wrong-headed animal had got there Megan could not guess, and still less did she know how to get it back. As there was no one else to talk to, she talked to herself. "Oh, dear, oh, dear, what shall I do?" she said.

"What is the matter, Megan?" said a voice behind her.

She turned round and saw a man cowled like a monk and with a rosary at his belt. She had not heard anyone coming, but the noise of the waters boiling over and through the rocks, she reflected, might easily have drowned the sound of any footsteps.

And in any case she was so troubled about her cow that she could not stop to wonder how the stranger had come up.

"I am ruined," said Megan. "There is my one and only cow, the sole support of my old age, on the other side of the river, and I don't know how to get her back again. Oh, dear, oh, dear, I am ruined."

"Don't you worry about that," said the monk, "I'll get her back for you."

"How can you?" asked Megan, greatly surprised.

"I'll tell you," answered the stranger. "It is one of my amusements to build bridges, and if you like I'll throw a bridge across this chasm for you."

"Well, indeed," said the old woman, "nothing would please me better. But how am I to pay you? I am sure you will want a great deal for a job like this, and I am so poor that I have no money to spare, look you, no, indeed."

"I am very easily satisfied," said the monk. "Just let me have the first living thing that crosses the bridge after I have finished it, and I shall be content."

Megan agreed to this, and the monk told her to go back to her cottage and wait there until he should call for her.

Now, Megan was not half such a fool as she looked, and she had noticed, while talking to the kind and obliging stranger, that there was something rather peculiar about his foot. She had a suspicion, too, that his knees were behind instead of being in front, and while she was waiting for the summons she thought so hard that it made her head ache. By the time she was halloed for, she had hit upon a plan. She threw some crusts to her little dog to make him follow her, and took a loaf of bread under her shawl to the river-side.

"There's a bridge for you," said the monk, pointing proudly to a fine span bestriding the yawning chasm. And it really was something to be proud of.

"H'm, yes," said Megan, looking doubtfully at it; "yes, it is a bridge. But is it strong?"

"Strong?" said the builder, indignantly. "Of course it is strong."

"Will it hold the weight of this loaf?" asked Megan, bringing the bread out from underneath her shawl.

The monk laughed scornfully. "Hold the weight of this loaf? Throw it on and see. Ha, ha!"

So Megan rolled the loaf right across the bridge, and the little black cur scampered after it.

"Yes, it will do," said Megan, "and, kind sir, my little dog is the first live thing to cross the bridge. You are welcome to him, and I thank you very much for all the trouble you have taken."

"Tut, the silly dog is no good to me," said the stranger, very crossly, and with that he vanished into space. From the smell of brimstone which he had left behind him Megan knew that, as she had suspected, it was the Devil whom she had outwitted.

And this is how the Bad Man's Bridge came to be built.

The Martyred Hound

PRINCE LLYWELYN had a favourite greyhound named Gelert that had been given him by his father-in-law, King John of England. He was as gentle as a lamb at home, but a lion in the chase, so true and so brave that he had no equal in the whole of his master's dominion. He fed only at Llywelyn's board and sentinelled Llywelyn's bed.

One fine morning the Prince determined to go to the chase, and blew his horn in front of the castle. All his other hounds came to the call, but Gelert did not answer it. He blew a louder blast on his horn and shouted, "Come, Gelert, come," saying to his huntsman that it was strange that Gelert should be the last to hear his horn. But still the greyhound did not come, and the chase had to ride on without him.

Llywelyn enjoyed the chase of hart and hare through the vales of Snowdon but little that day, and the booty proved scant and small because Gelert was not there. Disappointed and displeased he turned back to his castle, and as he came to the gate whom should he see but Gelert bounding out to greet him. When the hound came near him the Prince was startled to see that he was smeared all over with gore, and that his lips and fangs were dripping with blood. Llywelyn gazed at him with fierce surprise, and the greyhound crouched and licked his feet, as if surprised or afraid at the way his master received his greeting.

Now, Llywelyn had a little son about two years old with whom Gelert used to play, and the thought that the hound seemed guilty of something or other made him hurry towards the child's nursery, Gelert following at his heels. Entering, he saw the floor and walls besprent with recent blood, and, worst of all, the child's cradle was overturned; the coverlet was torn and all was daubed with blood. Llywelyn called his son, but no voice replied: he searched for him, wild with terror, but nowhere could he find him. He jumped to the conclusion that Gelert had destroyed his boy, and shouting, "Hell-hound, thou hast devoured my child," the frantic father drew his sword and plunged it to the hilt in the greyhound's side, who fell with a deep groan, gazing piteously in his master's eyes.

Gelert's dying groan was answered by a little child's cry from beneath the overturned cradle. There concealed beneath a tumbled heap which he had missed in his hurried search, Llywelyn found his little son unharmed and glowing from his rosy sleep. Just beside him lay the body of a great, gaunt wolf, all torn to pieces and stiff in death. Too late, Llywelyn realised what had happened while he was at the chase: Gelert had fought and slain the wolf which had come to destroy Llywelyn's heir.

In vain was all Llywelyn's grief: he could not bring his faithful hound to life again. So he buried him and raised a noble tomb over his bones, repenting his rashness with many tears. He could never bear the thought of the chase after this, and hung his horn and hunting spear at Gelert's grave. To this day the place is called Bedd Gelert, or the Grave of Gelert, and if you go there you will be shown the spot where the remains of the martyred hound lie.

Twm of the Fair Lies

THERE was once a man in South Wales who was fond of prophecy. He used to predict nice things for those who were kind to him, and nasty things for those who offended him. Now, very few of the pleasant things which he foretold came to pass, and so he got the name of Twm Gelwydd Teg, or Twm of the Fair Lies. But some of the unpleasant things which he said would happen to those who vexed him came true by some accident or other. Here is one of them. Sir George Herbert, of Cynfig Castle, once put him in prison, and Twm was very angry. After he came out of jail a great feast was held to celebrate the birth of a son and heir to Sir George. There was great rejoicing, and the proud father actually shod his horses with silver in honour of the event. When Twm heard of this, he said, "What a fuss about a baby which will be hanged by the string of its forehead-band." Sir George was told about this, and though he did not believe that Twm was a true prophet, still he thought that he could not be too careful. The child was placed under the charge of a nurse who was strictly ordered to watch him narrowly night and day. Everything went on all right for some time, but one day somebody told Sir George and his lady that the nurse had an infectious skin disease. They sent for her at once, but found that the woman's skin was as healthy as their own. They went back with her to the nursery, and the first thing they saw was the baby dead in the cradle. The forehead band had slipped down, and the child had twisted his hands in it in such a manner that he had choked and died.

Another time Twm was threshing corn in a barn. In came a young lad and addressed him: "Well, Twm Gelwydd Teg, what news have you to-day?" "I have news which concerns you," answered Twm. "You shall die three deaths before night." "Ha, ha," said the youth, "nobody can die more than one death," and he went off laughing.

In the course of the day the lad climbed to the top of a tall tree by the side of a river to rob a kite's nest. As he was thrusting his hand into the nest an adder stung him. He lost his hold and fell on a great branch, breaking his neck. Then his body fell into the river and sank into the depths of the water. He thus died three deaths: he was stung by an adder; he broke his neck; and he was drowned.

Black Robin

THERE was once an old man in North Wales called Robin Ddu, or Black Robin. He pretended to be a wizard, and though he had no magical power, he was so cunning that he made people believe he had, and his fame spread over the whole of Wales.

A lady in the Vale of Towy lost three precious gems. They had been given to her by a dead sister, and she valued them all the more on that account. Every search was made for them, but they could not be found. The lady had not heard of the Well of Llanbedrog—(by means of that it is quite easy to discover who has stolen your property. All you have to do is to kneel by it, and after throwing in a bit of bread name all whom you suspect. When the thief's name is mentioned the bread sinks)—but she had heard of Black Robin, and at last she decided to send for him. She despatched a servant to North Wales to offer him fifty pounds if he would restore her lost diamonds to her, and Robin travelled south with the messenger. When he arrived he said he would not begin his work unless fifty pounds were given to him beforehand. "Fifty pounds is a lot of money," said the lady. "I should like to test your power before giving it to you."

To this Robin reluctantly agreed. The lady put a tame robin redbreast under a dish on the table. Sending for the supposed magician, she asked him to say what was under the vessel. He did not know what to say or do, and thought the best thing he could do was to confess his ignorance. "Robin is caught," he said. Thinking he referred to the bird and not to himself, the lady was astounded at what she regarded as a wonderful display of power, and Robin was too cunning to confess. The money was paid over, and the process of finding the gems began.

First of all he inquired carefully into all the circumstances of the disappearance of the gems, cross-examining all the inmates of the house minutely. This investigation convinced him that one of the servants had stolen them, but for some time he could not find out the actual thief. One day, as he was taking the air with one of the men-servants, he happened to enter the churchyard. The sexton in digging a grave had come across a quantity of old bones, among them being a skull. Robin took the skull back with him to his room, and his startled companion told the servants' hall about it. Then Robin called all the servants to him, and looking very stern, "To-morrow night," said he, "I will summon a legion of devils, and they will punish the guilty with all the tortures of hell. But the innocent shall not suffer with the guilty. Take these," and with this he handed to each a tooth which he had wrenched from the skull. "By Friday morning" (it was then Wednesday) "the guilty, after suffering unspeakable anguish and pain, will be as dead as the body from which these teeth have been taken. But I will not invoke my devils if the gems are brought to me before midnight, nor will I disclose to any living soul who took them."

Sure enough, before midnight on Thursday a trembling maid-servant brought the diamonds to his room. The next thing to devise was how to restore them to their owner without disclosing the manner in which they had been recovered, and at the same time in such a way as to reflect credit on himself as a magician. Looking out of his window in the morning he saw a flock of geese feeding in a field not far from the mansion. Going out he took with him a small piece of bread, in which he placed the stones. He threw the piece of bread to the gander, which at once greedily swallowed it. Some time after, summoning the lady, "Kill that gander," he said, "and you will find inside him your lost treasure." This was done and the diamonds were found. "They were dropped on the floor and accidentally swept out with the dust," he explained, "and this greedy bird swallowed them. By means of the skull which the sexton dug out of the grave on Wednesday I was able to divine the mystery."

Llyn Llech Owen

THERE was a man living on Mynydd Mawr, in Carmarthenshire, who had a magic well. Over this he kept a large flat stone, which he was always careful to replace over its mouth after he had satisfied himself or his beast with water.

One summer evening Owen Glyndwr was passing through these parts of the ancient kingdom of South Wales, and he and his horse were weary and spent. He chanced upon this well, and removing the covering stone, drank long and deep draughts of the bubbling fountain, and gave to his parched steed. He then went on his way, without sealing the spring, and lodged for the night at Dyllgoed Farm close by. In the night he was awakened by the sound of flowing waters, and looking out saw a dark lake where the emerald meadows had smiled, white with flocks. Saddling his horse, he rode round the flood, and the horse's track in galloping round the water put a stop to its further overflow. This is the origin of Llyn Llech Owen, the Lake of Owen's Flag.

A Ghostly Rehearsal

WHILE the Manchester and Milford railway was being constructed, many a frugal farmer added to his earnings by boarding and lodging the navvies who were exalting the valleys and making low the hills for the iron rails. Several of these sturdy workers stayed at a farm called Penderlwyngoch.

One evening when they were seated round the fire in the big kitchen smoking and yarning, the farm dogs were heard barking, as they always did when they saw strangers anywhere about. As they continued to bark, the company understood that someone was coming towards the house. By-and-by they heard the sound of footsteps, and the barking of the dogs changed into a melancholy howl. Shortly after the howling ceased, as if the dogs had slunk away. Before many minutes had elapsed the back door opened, and a number of people entered the house: they passed along the passage which divided the dwelling into two parts, and laid a heavy load in the parlour: after this the noise suddenly stopped altogether.

The attention of the smokers would have been arrested by the mere opening of the parlour door. It was no light matter to burst into the musty splendour of the room where the sacred horsehair furniture and the family Bible were kept. There was, besides, something uncanny about the silence of the dogs and the sudden cessation of all noise in the parlour, which disturbed the company assembled in the kitchen. They took a light and proceeded to the parlour to investigate. There was nothing beyond what was always there, nor were there any marks of footsteps either in the room or in the passage. Going outside, they could find no traces of the approach of anyone, but they saw the dogs cowering and shivering with fright in the yard.

On the very next day one of the men who went to see what was the matter in the parlour was killed. His body was carried by his fellow-workmen through the back door and the passage which divided the house into the parlour. Everything occurred as it had been rehearsed the previous night except that the dogs were not frightened by the real corpse.

A Phantom Funeral

THE HARVEST of 1816 was one of the wettest ever known in Wales. In the evening of a day which had been comparatively dry a man and his wife, who lived in the Hundred of Moeddin, in Cardiganshire, went out to bind into sheaves some corn which had long been reaped and was lying on the ground. It was a beautiful evening, and the harvest moon was shining brightly.

The field in which they worked had the parish road passing along one of its sides, without a hedge or a ditch to separate it from the corn. When they had been busy for half-an-hour or more, they heard the hum of voices, as if of a crowd of people coming along the road leading past the field. They paused in their work and, looking in the direction of the sounds, they saw in the golden light of the moon a multitude of men and women coming into sight and advancing towards them. Being very intent upon their work, they again bent them to their task, without thinking much about what they had heard and seen; for they fancied, so far as they reflected over the matter at all, that some belated travellers were making their way to the village, which was about a mile off.

But the confused hum grew louder, and when the two binders looked up again they beheld a large crowd approaching gradually nearer. This time they continued to gaze at the assemblage, and they beheld quite clearly a coffin on a bier, carried on the shoulders of men, who were relieved by others in turn, as is usual in Cardiganshire funerals. "Here is a funeral," said the binders to one another, forgetting for the moment that it was not customary for funerals to be seen at night. They kept looking on till the crowd was right opposite them: some of them did not keep to the road, but walked over the corn alongside of the bulk of the procession. The binders heard the tramp of feet and the sound of voices, but not a syllable could they comprehend of what was said, not a face could they recognise. They kept their eyes on the procession till it went out of sight on the way leading towards the parish church. They saw no more of it, and an eerie feeling coming over them, they went home, leaving the corn on the ground.

Further on the funeral was met by a tailor at a point in the road where it was narrow and bounded by a fence on either side. The mourners filled the space from hedge to hedge, and when the tailor tried to force his way through, such was the pressure of the throng that he was obliged to get out of the way by crossing the hedge. He also failed to recognise any face, nor did he understand a word of the talk which he heard.

It was not, however, a real funeral: it was three weeks after this spectral funeral that the real one came down that way from the upper end of the parish.

Why the Robin's Breast Is Red

A WELSH boy was throwing stones one day at a robin red-breast. "My poor boy," said his grandmother to him, "have you not heard of the fiery pit and how this merciful bird takes cool dew on his little bill and lets it fall on sinful souls in torment? The marks of the fire that scorches him as he drops the water are to be seen on his red breast. Never throw a stone at a robin."